ε

"I Want You, Vanessa,

he muttered thickly.

His mouth moved roughly near her ear. His hands moved upward to caress her. There was an aching familiarity in his intimate caress, so arousing and possessive.

With forceful pressure, he turned her around and spread his hand over the side of her face. He crushed her pliant body to his, and kissed her with a deep, raw hunger that flamed through her blood. She was helpless to combat the fires he started. . . .

JANET DAILEY

having lived in so many locales, has come to know the people of America. She has written 65 books—selling over 80 million copies—and she'll be writing many more for Silhouette in the future. Her husband, Bill, is actively involved in doing all the research for Janet's books. They make their home in Branson, Missouri.

Dear Reader:

During the last year, many of you have written to Silhouette telling us what you like best about Silhouette Romances and, more recently, about Silhouette Special Editions. You've also told us what else you'd like to read from Silhouette. With your comments and suggestions in mind, we've developed SILHOUETTE DESIRE.

SILHOUETTE DESIREs will be on sale this June, and each month we'll bring you four new DESIREs written by some of your favorite authors—Stephanie James, Diana Palmer, Rita Clay, Suzanne Simms and many more.

SILHOUETTE DESIREs may not be for everyone, but they are for those readers who want a more sensual, provocative romance. The heroines are slightly older—women who are actively involved in their careers and the world around them. If you want to experience all the excitement, passion and joy of falling in love, then SILHOUETTE DESIRE is for you.

I'd appreciate any thoughts you'd like to share with us on new SILHOUETTE DESIRE, and I invite you to write to us at the address below:

Karen Solem
Editor-in-Chief
Silhouette Books
P.O. Box 769
New York, N.Y. 10019

JANET DAILEY
Wildcatter's Woman

Silhouette Romance
Published by Silhouette Books New York
America's Publisher of Contemporary Romance

Other Silhouette Books by Janet Dailey

The Hostage Bride
The Lancaster Men
For the Love of God
Terms of Surrender

SILHOUETTE BOOKS, a Simon & Schuster Division of
GULF & WESTERN CORPORATION
1230 Avenue of the Americas, New York, N.Y. 10020

ISBN: 0-671-57153-2

First Silhouette Books printing May, 1982

10 9 8 7 6 5 4 3 2 1

America's Publisher of Contemporary Romance

Printed in the U.S.A.

Wildcatter's
Woman

Chapter One

"Now, this pearl mist makes an interesting contrast to the Sudan green." Vanessa Cantrell laid the swatch of fabric against the square of thickly piled carpet so her client could study the combination together. "It would be an excellent complement to the patterned fabric you chose for the sofa."

"It is very attractive." But the young Mrs. Dumond, a recent bride, sounded uncertain. Her indulging husband, a well-established member of New Orleans society, wanted her to redecorate their home in the Garden District, but the young Mrs. Dumond, barely twenty years old, was intimidated by the responsibility, unsure of her taste.

It seemed Vanessa had to coax even the smallest decision from the girl. At twenty-eight, she felt very much that she was filling the role of an older sister instead of an interior decorator. It was a strain to be both.

A restless impatience stirred Vanessa as her young client wavered indecisively over the choices of fabric for the chair coverings. Long, curling lashes came down to conceal the flash of annoyance that darkened her violet eyes. Nodding an indefinite response to a meaningless comment, Vanessa let her glance stray to the French windows, laced with grillwork, and the private courtyard beyond them. It was lush and green out there—a riot of blossoming spring flowers. She could almost hear the tinkling melody of the water spilling over the sides of the mossy fountain.

She pulled her glance inside again and let it critically sweep the sitting room where she entertained her clients. It was flawlessly appointed, elegant with a discreet scattering of antiques. Lately, Vanessa had become dissatisfied with it. The room was so perfectly done that it lacked any life. It didn't reflect her personality —or perhaps it did. Regardless of the outward trappings of beauty, poise, and a successful career, inside there was a lot of emptiness when she should have felt fulfilled. She had achieved everything she wanted. She had security, a beautiful apartment in the French Quarter, and a smooth, orderly life-style. She virtually had her pick of eligible men, so she never lacked for male companionship. Yet . . .

The white enameled door connecting the sitting room with the offices swung partially open, the movement in her side vision attracting Vanessa's attention. She glanced at her secretary with a questioning look.

"Yes, Miss Austin, what is it?" The coolness of her voice held reproval. It was a rule that she not be interrupted when she was with a client.

"I beg your pardon, Mrs. Cantrell," her secretary murmured in apology. "But you have an urgent phone call."

A finely drawn brow shot up in sharp question as Vanessa eyed her usually unflappable secretary, who seemed rather worried. Her mind raced over the possibilities but couldn't find a plausible source for this "urgent" phone call. Turning a calm expression onto her client, Vanessa let a faint smile appear on her delicately curved lips.

"Would you excuse me for a moment, Mrs. Dumond?" she asked politely, rising from the lavender brocade sofa as she spoke. The young bride made an uncertain nod of permission, looking vaguely lost at the idea of being left alone.

Again, Vanessa quelled the unnatural rush of irritation as she glided across the room, her heels making little clicking sounds on glistening hardwood floor. She caught a glimpse of her reflection in the rococo wall mirror. It showed none of her inner restlessness and vague impatience, only satin brown hair sleeked away from her smooth, expressionless face into a French coil. It reminded Vanessa of the vacant, mannequin look of a model—beauty without any substance, like the room.

As soon as she pulled the door closed behind her, she sent a sharp look at her secretary. "Who is on the phone, Carla?" Carla Austin was the same age as Vanessa, but on the plain side, with a wallflower's ability to blend into the background. After four years, Vanessa had ceased trying to persuade Carla to choose a more flattering hairstyle, to wear a little more makeup, and to dress more fashionably. Carla simply did not want to stand out.

"It's Mrs. Devereux, your father-in-law's secretary." Carla Austin scanned Vanessa's face with an anxious look. "I'm . . . afraid it's bad news."

An unnamable fear gripped her throat, holding Vanessa motionless for a split second. She didn't even bother to correct Carla that it was her *ex*-father-in-law as she hurriedly crossed to her desk. Something must have happened to Race. Regardless of the bitter acrimony that had surrounded their divorce, there had been something between them once, so Vanessa told herself it was all right to be concerned for him at this moment.

Her hand trembled slightly as she lifted the receiver to her ear. "Mrs. Devereux? This is Vanessa." Divorce had ended her marriage to Race Cantrell four years ago, but it hadn't broken the close relationship with his father, Phillip Cantrell. He had sided with Vanessa in the divorce, blaming the reckless behavior of his son for the breakup. Phillip Cantrell had gladly assumed the role of father figure in her life, taking the place of her own parents, killed in a car crash when Vanessa was sixteen.

"Vanessa." There was a desperate ring in the woman's voice that seemed to reach through the phone lines. "There's no easy way to say this." Sybil Devereux's voice wavered. "Phillip has had a heart attack. A mild one, the doctor said, but . . . Please, he wants to see you."

"I'll come immediately." The first breath of relief that it wasn't Race quickly fled when the realization sank in that it was his father. Panic churned in her stomach at the phrase "heart attack." "Which hospital?"

Not trusting her memory, Vanessa jotted down the hospital on a notepad and tore off the sheet. As she hung up the phone, she was mentally trying to estimate how long it would take her to reach the hospital in the city traffic.

"Is your father-in-law very bad?" Carla murmured with concern.

"I don't know." Vanessa kept her inner apprehensions contained, but it was difficult to regard any heart attack as mild. "He's in the intensive-care unit. I'm going there now."

"What about Mrs. Dumond?"

Vanessa had forgotten about the young woman waiting in the sitting room. Agitation darkened the violet color of her eyes. "Is Peter free?" She demanded to know the status of her assistant, recently hired to keep pace with her expanding trade.

Peter Benoit, or Pierre as he was known to his clients, had previously had his own decorating shop. A creative genius with colors and fabrics, he totally lacked any business sense. When his shop failed six months ago, he had readily offered his talents to Vanessa's flourishing business.

"Yes. He's in his office. Shall I get him for you?" Carla offered.

"Just tell him to explain to Mrs. Dumond that I've been called away on a family emergency. Brief him on the color schemes and styles Mrs. Dumond has already chosen." While she gave the orders, Vanessa was collecting her purse and searching through the contents for her car keys. "And tell him not to let Mrs. Dumond select that brocade. It's much too dramatic and it wouldn't work at all."

"I will," Carla Austin promised. "Is there anything I can do to help?"

Vanessa paused to take a deep breath, then shook her head. "No. I don't know when I'll be back. I'll try to call."

"Shall I cancel your luncheon appointment?"

"Cancel all my appointments," she instructed, and walked swiftly to the shop's rear exit.

The traffic seemed abnormally heavy, although Vanessa suspected it was merely because she was in such a hurry. The air-conditioning of her car cooled the morning temperature but it alleviated little of the humidity. The teal-blue material of her blouse began sticking to her skin while the draping flare of her white skirt hugged her legs, as she alternately shifted her foot from the brake to the accelerator in the stop-and-go, bumper-to-bumper traffic.

Her concentration on driving was haunted by the image of Phillip Cantrell lying in a hospital bed surrounded by all sorts of tubes and monitors. Only last week she had lunched with her ex-father-in-law, a tall, distinguished banker. She owed him so much. It was his moral support that had helped her through the often cruel wrangling of the divorce proceedings. Later, his financial support had allowed her to start her own decorating business.

Not for the first time, Vanessa wondered how things might have turned out if Race had been more like his father. Both she and Phillip had believed Race would settle down after the wedding, but he hadn't. Vanessa had never been sure from one day to the next where he was or when he was coming home. There wasn't a dependable bone in his body. No matter how much she and Phillip argued with him, he had refused to change. He wouldn't give up the excitement, adventure, and risk of wildcatting for oil and gas.

The final straw had come when he had gambled everything they owned and more on a hole in the ground that came up dry. The day the court served papers on Vanessa to foreclose on their house and personal possessions, there had been a moment of hope that Race might have learned his lesson. But that hope was dashed to the ground when he came home that night and informed her he was leaving for Houston to meet a potential investor interested in buying into his next drilling venture.

The next day, Vanessa had gone to Phillip

Cantrell's attorney and had papers drawn up, suing for a divorce on the grounds of desertion, nonsupport, and mental cruelty. Looking back, she could see now that their problems had been more than financial ones. They were poles apart, wanting different things out of life. Vanessa craved security and a stable home life, probably because she had lost her parents at such a critical age. She liked beautiful things. Race cared about none of that. He was a loner, a gambler, self-sufficient, needing no one—as it turned out, not even Vanessa.

If there had been time, she probably would have seen it, but she had been blinded by his background. She had looked at Race's father, Phillip Cantrell, and seen a conservative, socially prominent man. Foolishly she had believed "like father, like son." His bold, reckless ways she had thought were just the sowing of wild oats before settling down. Within a month after meeting him, Vanessa became Mrs. Race Cantrell, and she discovered just how wrong she had been.

Reaching the hospital, Vanessa left the car in the parking lot and hurried into the main entrance. She paused at the information desk long enough to obtain directions to the intensive-care unit and inquire as to Phillip Cantrell's condition. She was not reassured by the information that he was listed in stable, although still-critical condition.

The high heels of her teal-blue shoes clicked noisily down the tiled hospital corridors. Vanessa slowed her pace as she neared the waiting room of the intensive-care unit. It suddenly occurred to her that Race was probably there. She had not seen him since their last bitter shouting match in divorce court four years ago. Nervous churnings began attacking her system.

Even though they both resided in New Orleans, it really wasn't so strange that their paths hadn't crossed. By choice, Race didn't travel in the same social circles as Vanessa or his father. In addition, Phillip's support of Vanessa's position had created an estrangement from his son, although Vanessa didn't believe the rift would keep Race away from his father's bedside. His work also kept him away from the city at various drilling sites or chasing down leases or investors. The rare times Vanessa had needed to communicate with Race, she had done it through her lawyer. The whole traumatic marriage/divorce experience had left her extremely wary of men and any kind of intimate relations with the opposite sex. Sometimes Vanessa felt she had survived only on the strength of pure, unadulterated hate.

She searched for that armor of violent emotion as she reached the doorway to the waiting room. There was only one occupant inside. Relief shivered through Vanessa as she recognized Sybil Devereux, Phillip's longtime friend and secretary. Sybil was an attractive widow in her early forties. Vanessa had always suspected that someday she and Phillip would marry. But, unlike his son, Phillip didn't rush into commitments without long and careful consideration.

"Vanessa . . ." Sybil's voice wavered on a sob

when she saw her. A shimmer of tears rimmed her dark eyes. "I'm so glad you're here."

"I came as soon as I could." Vanessa crossed the room to sit on the edge of the vinyl sofa next to the older brunette. "How is Phillip? Have you seen him?"

The woman dabbed at her eyes with a lace-edged handkerchief and tried to put on a brave face. "No. They're only allowing members of the family to see him. The doctor did tell me that his vital signs have stabilized, and he's responding to treatment."

"That's good news," Vanessa insisted in an effort to assure the woman and herself. Her glance strayed to the closed door across the hall from the waiting room, marked "ICU." An inner tension brought her teeth together. "Is Race with him?" There was an edge to her attempt at a bland inquiry.

"No." Sybil shook her head and breathed out a shaky sigh. "I haven't been able to contact him. He's out of the city. I left word with his secretary that it was urgent he contact me."

"Oh." It was a small sound of relief that she wouldn't have to be confronted by Race's presence, at least not right now. "Did you explain the urgency?"

"I . . . couldn't," Sybil admitted. "It seemed much too cold to leave a message that Phillip had suffered a heart attack. I couldn't be that blunt and unfeeling."

"I doubt if Race would have noticed," Vanessa replied with a dry note of sarcasm. He had never been one to cloak his remarks in gentle phrases.

16

Sybil Devereux wasn't listening, distracted by the appearance of a green-coated figure in the doorway. She rose anxiously to her feet. "How is he, Doctor?"

Turning, Vanessa slowly came to her feet while she studied the professional smile on the man's face, but his features showed no more than he wanted them to see. "He's doing very well under the circumstances, Mrs. Devereux."

"I'm Vanessa Cantrell," Vanessa identified herself when the doctor sent a questioning glance her way.

"I'm sorry." Sybil immediately apologized for not making the introduction sooner. "This is Mr. Cantrell's daughter-in-law, Dr. Foley." Then she explained to Vanessa, "Dr. Foley is the cardiologist."

"Vanessa?" He repeated her name on a slightly questioning note. "Mr. Cantrell has been asking for you. You may see him if you wish, but I must restrict your visit to a couple of minutes."

"Please, I'd . . . like to see him." She faltered a second, her voice choking up on a throb of concern.

The doctor must have read the silent plea in Sybil Devereux's expression, because he added, "I'm sorry, Mrs. Devereux, but only members of the family are allowed to see him. Perhaps tomorrow."

"Yes." It was a resigned answer as the older woman partially turned away. "I suppose I would be more useful at the bank than waiting here. I left everything in shambles when Phillip —Mr. Cantrell—started having chest pains during the board meeting. I . . ." Sybil paused to glance at Vanessa, her gaze clinging.

"I'll phone you the minute I know anything," Vanessa promised, and put an arm around the woman's shoulders to hug her briefly.

"If you'll come with me, Mrs. Cantrell . . ." the doctor prompted. After an exchange of strained smiles, Vanessa left the secretary to follow the doctor out of the waiting room into the intensive-care unit across the hall. "Have you managed to reach your husband yet, Mrs. Cantrell?" he inquired in a low voice.

She opened her mouth to explain their divorced status, then decided against it in case he wouldn't regard her as a family member. "Not yet," Vanessa murmured in an equally subdued voice.

When they stopped at Phillip's bedside, it was exactly the way she had envisioned it on the drive to the hospital. Intravenous tubes were feeding medication into his bloodstream. A string of wires hooked him up to the various monitoring machines beeping out his heartbeat and respiration rate. The oxygen tent enveloped him in a clear plastic cocoon. The streaks of gray in his dark hair seemed less distinguished and more an indication of his vulnerable years.

Tears raced into her eyes, despite her effort to blink them away. She started to reach for the white hand extruding from the plastic cocoon, then hesitated and glanced at the doctor. He silently nodded his permission. She curled her hand around the limp fingers.

"Phillip." There was a thready run in her

18

voice, and Vanessa paused to steady it. "It's me. Vanessa. I'm here, and everything's going to be all right."

With tears blurring her eyes, she was just able to see his faint stirring at the sound of her voice. His eyelids fluttered, briefly fighting the sedation. She saw his lips moving in a soundless effort to speak, but she couldn't make out what he was trying to say. She glanced mutely at the doctor.

"I believe he is asking for his son," the doctor guessed. "Is his name Pierce?"

"No, it's Race." But the two names would look similar when trying to read someone's lips, Vanessa realized. "He'll be here, Phillip," she insisted. "You rest for a while."

He appeared to relax, believing her, when she had no idea how long it might be before Race was notified about his father. The doctor touched her elbow to signify she had stayed long enough.

In the outer hallway again, the doctor stopped. "Perhaps you should try to contact your husband again, Mrs. Cantrell."

Something in his tone alarmed Vanessa. "Is Phillip's condition more serious than I was led to believe?"

"He is responding very well to the treatment, Mrs. Cantrell, but I don't want your father-in-law to be subjected to undue anxieties. I want him to stay as calm as possible. And I don't think that state is going to be achieved until he sees his son," the doctor explained.

"I understand," she murmured.

"There's a telephone in the waiting room you can use." He gestured in the general direction of the room.

While Vanessa hesitated, trying to find a way to explain why she didn't want to speak to Race, the doctor walked quietly away. She was glad, then, that she hadn't protested. Under the circumstances, it would have been petty. This wasn't the time to be concerned about her bitter differences with Race. Phillip wanted him here.

She entered the waiting room and walked straight to the telephone. The fat phone book sat on the lower shelf of the table where the phone rested. Pulling it out, Vanessa sat down on the straight chair and balanced the phone book on her lap. She flipped through the white pages to the back of the book and stopped to run her finger down the W section until she found the listing of Westcat Oil and Gas Company.

Ignoring the uneven murmuring of her heart, she dialed the number. There was a moistness in her palms as she held the receiver tightly and listened to the ringing on the other end of the line.

A woman's voice answered, "Good morning. Westcat. May I help you?"

Before Vanessa could respond, there was a partially muffled sound of laughter in the background. "I'd like to speak to Race Cantrell, please," Vanessa requested stiffly.

"I'm sorry, he isn't here." There was an underlining hint of laughter in the woman's voice that Vanessa resented. "May I give him a message?"

"When do you expect him?" she demanded.

20

"I don't expect Mr. Cantrell in the office for several days," was the reply. In the background, a man's voice murmured, "While the cat's away—" But the rest of his phrase was silenced by a loud "Sssh" by the woman on the phone. "However, he will be checking in with me."

"It's imperative that I speak to him right away," Vanessa asserted. "Is there another number where I could reach him?"

"No, I'm sorry. Mr. Cantrell is at one of the drilling sites. And there isn't any phone there," the woman explained. "If you would care to leave your name and a message, I can pass it on to him. He should be calling me this noon."

"Very well." Vanessa released a long breath. "Tell him that Vanessa called. Vanessa Cantrell. It's extremely urgent that I speak to him . . . on an important family matter." Like Sybil, she discovered that she was reluctant to flatly leave a message of Phillip's heart attack.

There was a slight pause before the woman came back on the line to ask, "You are his ex-wife?"

"Yes," she confirmed with a faint snap to her voice.

"Is there a number you wish to leave?" The woman didn't sound as friendly this time.

Vanessa gave her the number on the telephone in the waiting room. "I'll wait for his call. Please stress that it is an emergency when you give him my message."

"I will." But the woman sounded indifferent.

"Thank you." After hanging up the receiver, Vanessa discovered she was trembling. She

21

stared at the phone a moment longer, awash again with the bitter anger and hurt that had marked the end of her marriage.

She moved away from the telephone and took a seat on the sofa, forcing her thoughts to Phillip in an effort to rid herself of the bad taste left by old memories. A nurse stopped by the waiting room and gave Vanessa a cup of black coffee. She shrugged aside the suggestion to have lunch in the hospital cafeteria. She had no appetite for food, subconsciously choosing to stay close to the telephone in case Race called.

At one-thirty the doctor walked past, then retraced his steps to pause in the waiting-room doorway. "Have you spoken to your husband yet, Mrs. Cantrell?"

"No. I left word for him to call me here." Vanessa nodded to the silent telephone on the table.

He sighed heavily, a grimness tightening his mouth. "Maybe you should try him again." The grim line curved upward in a semblance of a smile before he continued down the corridor.

Moistening her dry lips, Vanessa glanced at the phone. It was well past the lunch hour. The woman had said Race would be calling around noon. Surely he had received her message by now, so why hadn't he phoned? After a minor debate whether to call now or wait a little longer, Vanessa walked to the phone and dialed the number from memory. The same woman's voice answered the phone.

"This is Vanessa Cantrell again," she said briskly. "Have you spoken to Race yet?"

There was a long hesitation. "Mrs. Cantrell, of course, I recognize your voice. How are you?" It was a falsely bright reply.

Vanessa recognized the stalling tactic. "Did Mr. Cantrell call you at noon?" she demanded.

"Well, yes, he did," the woman admitted with obvious reluctance.

"Did you give him my message?" Her fingers curled tighter around the telephone receiver.

"I did, Mrs. Cantrell," the woman insisted defensively. "Hasn't he called you?"

Anger began building up inside her, a slow simmer heating her temper. "I have the feeling that you know very well that he hasn't called," Vanessa accused.

"I gave him the message," the woman repeated.

"What did he say when you relayed it to him?" she asked, her suspicion growing into a certainty.

"Mrs. Cantrell, he made no reply whatsoever." Her answer was very definite.

"His father has had a heart attack." Vanessa ignored the gasp of dismay that came over the phone. "Now, will you tell me where I can find your employer? You said he was at a drilling site. Which one?"

"It's located in Assumption Parish. Mrs. Cantrell, there really isn't a telephone at the site," the woman inserted, in case Vanessa thought she had lied about that. "The best I can do is leave a message at the motel where he's staying, but I can't be sure when he would receive it."

Vanessa didn't need an explanation of that.

There had been many nights spent alone while they were married, with Race wandering in during the wee hours of the morning after working most of the night on drilling rigs. Once a well was spudded in, the drilling went on twenty-four hours a day as long as the money lasted.

"Don't bother," Vanessa replied. "I could probably drive there and back by the time he'd receive your message. Assumption Parish is near Thibodaux, isn't it?" In Louisiana, there were no counties. The state was sectioned into parishes.

"Yes, it's just northeast of Thibodaux."

"Give me directions to the drilling site." She opened her purse and took out a small notebook with a pen attached.

Chapter Two

The state road followed the meandering course of Bayou Lafourche, its banks clustered with homes belonging to a population of mainly Cajun fishermen working the shrimp fleets. Any other time, Vanessa would have found the drive picturesque, but she was tensely watching for her turnoff onto a side road. Even then, she almost missed it, seeing it at the last minute.

Within minutes, moss-draped trees increased in numbers on either side of the road. Vanessa slowed her silver-gray Porsche to read the last part of the directions again. The homes had thinned out, which meant fewer chances of asking directions.

Another three miles, she saw the sign she was looking for on a fence gate. It read: "Boar's Head

#1, Westcat Oil and Gas." She turned the car onto the narrow, rutted lane that led into the trees. She was nearly to the site before she could make out the skeletal steel of the drilling rig rising into the air.

There was little to distinguish this drilling site from hundreds of others Vanessa had seen when she reached it. A mud-spattered office trailer was parked to one side, with three equally dirty pickup trucks lined up in front of it. The drilling rig rose as high as the treetops, its pounding noise drowning out all other sounds in the quiet bayou country.

Vanessa stopped her car midway between the trailer and the drilling rig. Switching off the engine, she left the keys in the ignition and her purse on the passenger seat as she climbed out. Her high heels immediately sank into the soft earth, drawing an impatient curse as she quickly picked her way to drier ground. There was little of it in this low-lying area.

A man stepped out of the trailer and swung off the high step onto the ground. His muscled, chunky body was clad in a sweat-stained white T-shirt and khaki drill pants. He wore boots and a hard hat, typical of the half-dozen or so other workers on the rig. The man came to an abrupt stop, halting like a statue at the sight of the chicly dressed brunette in her white skirt and teal-blue blouse.

"Is Race Cantrell in the trailer?" Vanessa shouted, not wanting to ford the mud-puddle-strewn ground between herself and the trailer if he wasn't.

The man cupped a hand to his ear to indicate he couldn't hear above the noise of the drilling rig. The throbbing din was eroding her already thin control. Vanessa took a deep breath, fighting down the waves of irritation, and cupped both hands to her mouth to form a megaphone and shouted her question again. This time the roughneck shook his head in a negative answer and pointed toward the rig.

Turning, but being careful to keep to her patch of dry ground, Vanessa scanned the workers on the rig, trying to pick out Race from among them. With everyone in hard hats, it was difficult to distinguish one from another. Impatiently she began picking her way toward the rig, forced to watch the marshy ground if she wanted to avoid ruining her shoes.

A couple of shrill wolf whistles pierced the pulsating din of the drill being driven into the ground. Vanessa paused to look up and get her bearings. The rig floor was roughly ten feet above ground level with a set of steps allowing access.

Two men stood near the top of them, both half-turned toward her. Despite the distance and the hard hat that shaded most of his face, Vanessa recognized Race's tall, flatly muscled figure, instantly identifying him as the man on the right. It was something in his stance—in the way he carried himself—that always suggested latent power concealed behind loose-limbed ease. She noticed it now and could almost feel his gaze boring into her. Her pulse began to beat loudly in her ears, as if suddenly trying to compete with the rhythmic hammering of the drill. For a split second she wanted to turn and get as far away from him as possible. Then she remembered her purpose in coming and squared her shoulders on a determined angle.

Vanessa didn't have to be an expert in lip-reading to understand the order Race gave the man at his side. He was being told to "Get her out of here," and it was emphasized by the dismissing jerk of his hand. Her lips were compressed into a thin, tight line as Vanessa started forward again.

Before she reached the bottom of the steps, she was met by the man Race had sent to intercept her. Somewhere in his mid-thirties, the same age as Race, he was easily six feet, although not as tall as Race. His expression was decidedly unfriendly as he gripped her arm in his gloved hand and propelled her around to head back the way she'd come.

"This is a restricted area," he informed her coldly. "No unauthorized personnel are allowed. You'll have to leave."

Vanessa didn't attempt to struggle until she had solid ground under her feet. Her initial acquiescence had lulled the man into thinking she wasn't going to argue. Surprise flashed across his face when she suddenly stopped and pulled her arm free of his loose hold. She was doing a slow boil at Race's high-handed attempt to send someone else to get rid of her. An amethyst fire glittered in her eyes when she turned on him.

"I'm not going anywhere," she warned. "So

you can march right back up there on that rig and tell that to your boss."

"This is a hard-hat area—" the man began in tight-lipped protest.

"Then I'll wait in the trailer." Vanessa cut across his sentence and swung away to stalk across the moisture-laden ground.

Another worker was just coming out of the trailer as Vanessa reached it. There was a quagmire of mud directly beneath the metal step. If the worker hadn't extended a helping hand to pull her onto the high step, she doubted if she could have bridged the mud and kept her balance. She was too incensed to do more than nod a curt thanks for the assistance and ignore the slightly lascivious rake of the worker's glance as she brushed past him on the narrow flight of steps to go inside.

The long trailer was a combination of office, rec room, and bunkhouse all in one. The closed door shut out much of the drilling noise, creating a modicum of quiet. While the trailer offered a break from the glaring sun, it didn't lessen the oppressive humidity. A rotating fan whirred in the corner, circulating the heavy air.

Vanessa barely had time to glance around the cluttered jumble before the door opened behind her and the man who had attempted to escort her off the drilling site entered. Conscious that a display of temper would not accomplish any purpose, Vanessa tried to hold it in check.

"Would you please inform Race that it's imperative that I speak with him?" she requested with tautly coached politeness.

The man's glance touched her briefly and coolly, but he made no immediate response. He crossed the narrow width of the trailer and stopped in front of a tall avocado-green coffee urn sitting on a water-stained table. With growing irritation Vanessa watched him slide a white cup under the spigot and fill it with thick black coffee. He partially turned to look at her and lifted the cup to his mouth, taking a sip of it. With deliberate rudeness, he failed to offer her a cup of coffee.

"Race is busy," he finally responded to her request. "You can leave a message and I'll give it to him later."

"Oh, no," Vanessa breathed in angrily. "I didn't come all this way from New Orleans to be pawned off on some underling."

"That's your problem, Mrs. Cantrell—not mine," he replied with bland indifference.

She stiffened when he said her name, suddenly realizing the cause for his hostile attitude. "You men are always closing ranks to protect one another. Because I'm the ex-wife, that automatically makes me the villain of the piece, is that it?" she challenged.

"I wouldn't know, Mrs. Cantrell." He took another sip of his coffee.

"Look, Mr. . . . whoever you are . . ."

"Jeb Bannon," he supplied his name.

"Look, Mr. Bannon," Vanessa picked up where she'd left off, her voice trembling with anger, "I don't know why you think I'm here, but I've driven all this way to let Race know that—"

The door opened, letting in all the outside

noise. Vanessa swung around at the interruption to face the door. Her angry outburst was stopped cold by the unexpected appearance of Race. For the span of a hard-hitting second, there was a lock of clashing glances and no movement.

Some half-remembered sensation quivered through her nerve ends as his glance broke from hers. The door was shut with a decisive click. Vanessa hadn't expected four short years to make any changes in him, but they had. She began noticing the small differences the minute Race pulled off his hard hat with its decal of a snarling wildcat. There had always been the reckless glitter of wanderlust in his brown eyes, but that dark gleam had hardened with cynicism—a cynicism that had etched deeper lines in his sun-browned face, giving his lean male features a certain harshness. Maturity and experience had marked him with invisible scars of battles lost, but Vanessa sensed Race was the stronger for it and would ultimately win the war.

The hard hat was hooked on a wall peg and left to hang there as Race crossed to the coffee urn, peeling off his gloves and slapping them down on the table. He combed his fingers through the thickness of his dark, nearly black hair, carelessly rumpling it.

"I want to look over the well log, Jeb." Clean cups were overturned on a coffee-stained cloth. Race took one of them and righted it, filling it with coffee from the urn's spigot.

As the second man in the trailer went to retrieve the electrical record of the geological formations penetrated by the well, Vanessa realized that Race had not addressed a single word to her. That one glance when he came into the trailer had been the only time he acknowledged her presence. Resentment bristled along her spine at the way he was ignoring her. When the two men huddled in front of a littered desk to pore over the records, Vanessa stalked to the side of the desk to forcibly intrude.

"Pretending I'm not here won't make me go away, Race Cantrell." She curled her fingernails into her palms.

There was a brief silence, during which he didn't look up, not even when he finally spoke. "That would be wishful thinking, I suppose." The dryness of his tone was cutting.

It hurt. Even after all this time, she was still sensitive to his barbed remarks. "I had forgotten how rude and insulting you can be," Vanessa declared with a traitorous quiver to her chin. "I don't know why I bothered to come all the way out here."

Bending slightly at the waist, Race leaned both hands on the desktop, as if still intent on the well log. "I'll take it from here, Jeb." The hardness of steel ran beneath the casual tone that dismissed the second man.

As he moved away from the desk, Jeb Bannon downed the rest of his coffee in one gulp and threw Vanessa a flickering glance. The air inside the trailer was thick with hostility. She could feel it pressing in around her as the second man left his cup by the coffee urn and walked out the door.

After he was gone, Race remained in the same

position. Vanessa had a slim view of his craggy profile, but mostly her view was restricted to his back. The heat of a Louisiana afternoon had plastered the blue chambray shirt to his muscled skin, making her conscious of the tapering width of his shoulders.

"Will you look at me?" Vanessa demanded. "I don't like talking to people's backs."

She watched the rippling interplay of muscle and sinew as Race slowly straightened and turned at right angles to face her. His hard, flat gaze was unnerving. It was like coaxing a tiger close to the bars of its cage for a better look, then not feeling safe.

"Make it quick. I happen to be busy," Race snapped with a bored and impatient expression.

In defense, Vanessa resorted to sarcasm. "I know. You were so busy you couldn't take three minutes to return my call."

There was a curling lift of his mouth. "That's right," he agreed. "I had better things to do with my time than listen to you bitch because you haven't received your alimony check for three months. When I get the money, you'll be paid, although, judging by that shiny Porsche parked outside and"—his raking glance swept her from head to toe with insulting thoroughness—"the way you're dressed, you don't appear to be suffering any hardship."

The anger she'd been fighting so hard to contain bubbled over. "I'm glad you noticed that I don't have to depend on you to support me! If I had to rely on you, I wouldn't even have a roof over my head!" It was a deliberately cutting reminder that his financial gambles had cost them their home. A leaping fire blazed in his dark eyes as his jaw worked convulsively in anger. Shaken by the sensation that he was looming closer, when he hadn't even moved, Vanessa took a step backward and came up against the trailer wall.

"I could always count on your understanding, couldn't I?" Race jeered with contempt. "Times got a little rough, and you got going, taking everything that was left with you, and demanding alimony besides."

"You *owed* me that much." Her angry voice wavered with the strain of keeping its volume down, so this wouldn't turn into another one of their shouting matches. "And I certainly put the money to better use than you would have. You'd have poured it into another dry hole in the ground and lost it all."

In one step Race eliminated the small space that separated them. Vanessa flattened herself against the wall in sudden alarm. She was trapped, his hands pressed against the wall on either side of her while he towered inches from her. Taut rage marked his stillness as he glared down on her. She could feel the heat of his body down her whole length.

An awareness of his potent masculinity flooded through her. Race Cantrell was all man, a fact she had ignored in her anger. But having him this close to her again, it was brought sharply home. She couldn't draw a breath without drinking in his musky scent, so she didn't breathe, fighting off the pull of his male sexuality that had undermined her will so many times.

His gaze burned over her face with searing contempt. "What did I ever see in a money-grubbing bitch like you?" he muttered through clenched teeth.

The hot moistness of his breath fanned her cheeks, and Vanessa turned her face partially from him. She hated the weakness that was spreading through her limbs. Her stomach churned with the emotional turmoil of this violently charged scene. What was she doing here? Why hadn't she stayed away from him?

Then the reason pushed its way forward. "I didn't come here because of the alimony," she began stiffly. "I don't care if you pay it or not. I don't need it anymore. That wasn't why I wanted to talk to you."

"Really?" Race taunted, watching her lips with cold interest.

"It's your father." The hesitancy in her voice shifted his attention, his gaze narrowing as it met hers.

"Did he send you here?" Cynicism coated his question. The divorce had created a rift between father and son, Vanessa knew, but since she never talked about Race or even mentioned his name to Phillip, she wasn't sure of their present relationship—whether there might have been some tentative bridging.

"No. Not exactly," Vanessa qualified her answer slightly, compassion filling her expression to drive out the anger and bitterness. "Your father had a heart attack this morning, Race." His flatly muscled chest expanded with a quickly indrawn breath, although there was little change in his expression except for the probing search of his gaze for more information. "He's been asking for you," Vanessa explained.

He shoved away from the wall, turning to take a step toward the desk. "How serious is it?" he questioned without looking at her.

"It was classified as a mild attack. His condition had stabilized when I left," she replied. "I'm sorry, Race." She wasn't sure if it was an expression of sympathy or an apology for raking up the past. "I probably should have made the message more clear, but it seemed too brutal and inhuman to simply leave word that Phillip had suffered a heart attack."

"What brought it on? Do you know?" Race moved some papers around on the desk, expressing only mild interest.

"Not definitely, no." Vanessa frowned, confused by his cool attitude. "I only spoke to Mrs. Devereux briefly. I think it happened at the bank while he was attending a board meeting." Her frown deepened. "You will go see him?"

"Yes." He threw her a dry look over his shoulder. "Isn't that why you came? Or were you hoping to prove you were right when you claimed I had oil running through my veins?"

Vanessa had forgotten she had once accused him of that. All desire to argue with him had gone, so she didn't make any comment to his baiting questions.

"I take it that you'll be going to the hospital

when you get back to New Orleans," Race guessed.

"Yes," she confirmed.

"Any objections if I ride with you?" he challenged with an arched brow. Without giving her a chance to answer, Race continued on a caustically mocking note. "I'm sure it won't come as any surprise to you if I admit I can't afford the gasoline for the trip. This exploratory well has got me in hock up to my neck."

"It's no surprise." Her shoulders sagged with the flatness of her voice. In that respect, Race hadn't changed. He might be tougher, but he still was broke. If it wasn't for his father, Vanessa told herself, she'd inform Race he could hitch a ride with his thumb. "You can ride with me." But she was dreading the prospect of that much time in his company. She wasn't sure if her frayed nerves could stand it.

"Let's go, then." The grimness in his expression seemed to reflect her own feelings.

Race was already halfway to the door before Vanessa moved away from the wall. With a lack of gentlemanly courtesy, he walked out of the office trailer ahead of her and descended the metal steps, swinging off the last one to splash through the mud below it toward the pickup trucks. Jeb Bannon was leaning against the nearest one, smoking a cigarette. He ground it into the ground beneath his boot heel when Race approached, his glance flicking to Vanessa as she appeared in the doorway.

The incessant pounding of the drilling rig with its powerful motor covered the brief exchange of conversation between Race and the second man. Vanessa imagined Race was informing the man that he was leaving. She hesitated on the last step, trying to judge how far she had to jump to land on relatively solid ground. Not for anything was she going to ask Race to help her.

But he was already sloshing through the mud to the steps. The sardonic light in his dark eyes mocked her predicament as a hand reached for her waist. She laid a steadying hand on his shoulder and braced herself to be swung off the step onto the ground. Instead of his hands spanning her waist to lift her down, they scooped her into his arms. She went stiff with shock at this unexpected contact with his hard, muscled torso. His physical strength was evident in the ease with which he carried her, flexed muscles making their imprint felt on her flesh. She was prickled by slivers of unwanted sensations, close enough to make out each individual sun-crease fanning out from the corners of his eyes.

"High heels are not practical footwear at a drilling site—or white skirts, for that matter," Race observed dryly.

"But it isn't on my list of frequently visited places, either," she retorted as she realized he intended to carry her all the way to the car.

"That's true enough," he agreed with bitter grimness. "Even when we were married, you didn't visit me on the sites but a couple of times."

Vanessa bridled at the thinly veiled criticism. "I suppose you condemn me for that. If you loved me at all, you would have missed me enough to come home once in a while."

The roughnecks on the drilling rig howled wolf calls, seeing something suggestively intimate in the sophisticated brunette being carried to her sleek sports car. It increased the discomfort Vanessa was experiencing in the strong cradle of his arms. The sensation was becoming too familiar. To combat it, she averted her gaze from his virile features to look ahead. The silver-gray Porsche was only a couple of yards away.

Race stopped by the driver's side, keeping a steadying arm around her waist while he let her feet slide to the ground. The instant she had her balance, Vanessa pushed away from the lean strength of his body, wanting no more contact with it. She was already aware of the rapid patter of pulse in her neck. She wanted her sexual attraction for him to be as dead as her love was, but she was slowly recognizing that it wasn't as discriminating in its interest.

"Do you want to drive?" Vanessa asked, remembering that he had never allowed her behind the wheel if they were going together.

"It's your car." It was a hard smile. "You drive."

While she slid into the driver's seat, Race walked around to the passenger side and climbed in, shoving her purse onto the floor. It felt odd to have him be the one sitting idly by the right window as she started the car.

"Is this a vote of confidence?" Vanessa challenged, unable to let the milestone pass without comment. "You never used to trust me to drive you anywhere."

"Does it matter?" Race countered with a trace of sharpness, then adjusted the passenger seat to a reclining position. "If you don't mind, I'd just as soon skip the small talk and catch some sleep instead."

She shot a surprised glance at him, but his eyes were already closed, shutting her out somehow. His forehead was creased with weary lines, but it didn't lessen the rawness she felt. As she turned the car onto the rutted lane leading away from the drilling site, Vanessa swallowed the bitter taste of irony. She should be feeling relief that there wouldn't be any need to make stilted conversation, instead of feeling deprived of his company. Maybe she was feeling slighted because it was so typical of what their married life had been like—thus a painful reminder.

Vividly she recalled the rare times Race had spent at home. He had usually been too tired to go anywhere, and he had despised social gatherings anyway. If he wasn't in bed sleeping, he had usually been trying to persuade her to go to bed with him. The little talking they did was usually to quarrel about money.

It really wasn't surprising that the marriage had failed. Sometimes Vanessa wondered how it had lasted two years. It had been a mistake from the start.

As she entered the outskirts of New Orleans, Vanessa noticed the needle of the gas gauge was hovering on the empty mark. From experience, she knew it meant exactly what it said. There was a service station on the corner of the intersection just ahead. She flipped on the turn signal and stole a glance at Race.

His long frame was wedged sideways in the seat, his head resting against the passenger door. The shallowness of his breathing confirmed he was sleeping, but she didn't see how it was possible in such an uncomfortable position. Even in sleep, Race didn't look vulnerable. The male strength was still there, with only some of the harsh cynicism erased from his sun-lined features.

When she slowed the car to turn into the service station, Race stirred at the changing rhythm of the engine. As the car's motion ceased altogether, he wakened and sat up stiffly, flexing cramped muscles.

"I have to get gas." Vanessa explained the obvious and switched off the engine.

Race nodded wearily, haggard lines etched deeper in his face. Stretching out his right leg, he reached a hand inside his pants pocket. "I think I'll use the pay phone inside to call the hospital," he said.

The service-station attendant paused beside the driver's door while Vanessa rolled the window down. "Fill it up, please," she requested, then glanced at Race. "Will you hand me my purse?"

It was on the floor near his feet. Race extracted a coin from the handful of small change and shoved the rest back in his pocket before passing the purse to her. Vanessa stayed in the car while he went inside the building to make the call. Using the rearview mirror, she freshened her lipstick and tried to tuck the wisps of silky brown hair back into place.

By the time Race had returned, the tank had been filled with gas and Vanessa had paid the attendant. Race slid into the passenger side and sent a short glance to her.

"I spoke to the doctor, and he's doing fine," he stated.

"Good." She meant that, but she was also conscious that these were the first truly civil words they had exchanged.

"Since there isn't a critical need to get to the hospital immediately, I'd like to stop by my apartment so I can shower and change clothes before I see him. It won't take more than twenty minutes at the outside."

A ripple of tension traveled along her spine. It wasn't an unfair request, yet instinct advised her to refuse it. But she couldn't blame him for not wanting to go to the hospital in his work-clothes and smelling of perspiration.

"What's the address?" she asked briskly.

Chapter Three

"No one would mistake it for the St. Charles," Race commented wryly when Vanessa parked the car in front of the building address he'd given her.

The two-story red-brick building showed signs of disrepair. The ornamental grillwork was rusting in places and the white paint trimming the windows had started to crack and chip. Grass was growing up through the cracks in the sidewalk. It was representative of several New Orleans neighborhoods that suffered from neglect.

"Would you rather wait for me in the car or come inside?" he asked as he reached for the door handle.

"I'll come in with you." Whether she was willing to admit it or not, Vanessa was curious to see where he lived. A little late, she realized Race hadn't exactly invited her. "If you don't mind." She tacked the last on as an afterthought.

His shoulders lifted in a shrug of indifference. "I wouldn't have asked, if I did." Without waiting for her final decision, Race climbed out of the car.

Vanessa hesitated only a second longer before stepping out her side and walking around the hood to follow him up the sidewalk to the main door. Pushing it open, he entered ahead of her and held the door until she was through. With a gesture of his hand he indicated the shadowed staircase leading to the second floor. Vanessa climbed them a step ahead of Race.

A dark-haired woman in a skimpy sundress lounged in the doorway of the apartment at the head of the stairs. Big blue eyes swept insolently over Vanessa before swinging their attention to Race. A lazily sexy smile curved her full red lips.

"Race, honey, you got any cold beer?" she drawled.

"Sure." There was a jingle of keys as he stepped past Vanessa and moved to the door catty-corner across the hall from the brunette. "I always keep a supply of cold beer on hand, Marie. You know that," Race chided the woman, his glance raking her well-endowed figure with appreciative boldness before sliding mockingly to Vanessa.

With sickening resentment Vanessa was aware that Race had shared more than the same

apartment building and a few beers with the
sultry brunette. He unlocked the door and
pushed it open to let Vanessa enter.

It was a small, efficiency-type apartment with
a kitchen area occupying one wall. Vanessa
moved tensely into the center of the main room,
breathing in the staleness of the air that reeked
of unemptied ashtrays and dust. The refrigerator in the corner was an ancient white one. Race
walked over to it and opened the door.

"How many do you want, Marie?" He glanced
toward the hallway door. Vanessa swung partially around to see his sexy neighbor posing in the
doorway.

"Just a couple," the brunette replied, wrin-
kling her nose and somehow managing to make
the grimacing expression appear sexy. He took
two brown beer bottles from the refrigerator and
crossed the room to give them to Marie.
"Thanks, Race. And I'm really sorry about in-
truding when you're entertaining."

Liar, Vanessa thought viciously.

Race slid a cynically laughing glance at Vanessa. "I'm not exactly 'entertaining,' Marie,"
he corrected his neighbor. "My ex-wife is just
doing a bit of slumming."

"Oh." The amused look Marie gave her flamed
Vanessa's imagination with the one-sided tales
Race had probably told her. Then Marie was
smiling at him again. "If you get bored, you
know where I am." With feline grace she moved
out of the doorway, to disappear into the hallway.

Race appeared to watch her until she was out of his sight, then slowly closed the door and turned. Vanessa was trembling with some violent emotion that she refused to name. It darkened her eyes to a deep purple that glittered with angry sparks.

"A friend of yours?" Her voice was cloyingly sweet, sugar laced heavily with arsenic.

"Now, how did you guess?" he mocked. "I'd offer you a beer, but I know you hate the stuff. And I don't keep wine on hand. I've developed a strong aversion to it—and to women who like it."

It was a stab at her, since wine was usually the only alcoholic beverage she drank. She winced inwardly at the sharp sting of rejection. Why did he still have the power to hurt her?

"It's obvious that Marie likes beer." The sharp edge stayed in her voice, despite her attempt to sound indifferent. Vanessa swung her gaze away from Race, fighting to keep the cool mask in place and hide the churning conflict within. "How nice that you share the same taste."

"That's more than you and I could say—on just about everything." There was a deliberately unkind note of derisive amusement in his reply. "I like my beer, and you won't drink anything but wine. I'm happy with boiled shrimp, while you want oysters Rockefeller. The list is endless, so rather than continue in that 'happy' vein, I'll just go take my shower and change. I'd suggest that you make yourself comfortable, but I know this place isn't up to your standards."

For the first time, Vanessa took a really close

look at the apartment and its furnishings. Ignoring the surface clutter of discarded clothes, beer bottles, unemptied ashtrays, and scattered trade journals and newspapers, it had all the personality of a hotel room. It was colorless and lifeless.

"It hardly matters, since I don't have to live here," she retorted, giving the answer he expected to hear.

"It doesn't look like much," Race admitted without apology. "But the rent's cheap and it came furnished. It's just a place to sleep."

"That's all you ever wanted," Vanessa accused in a burst of bitterness. "A place to sleep, and a woman to bed whenever the urge struck you. With Marie just across the hall, now you have both."

His expression became complacently aloof as he regarded her with lazy interest. "You sound just like the wronged woman, Vanessa." It was the first time he'd spoken her name, and it curled around her throat. "You divorced me. Remember?" Race taunted, one corner of his mouth lifting.

She whirled away from him, something shattering inside and releasing a torrent of pain. "It was probably the only intelligent thing I've ever done." But she had to force the assertion past the huge lump in her throat. "Hadn't you better take your shower?" Her control was slipping away fast.

"Yeah." It was a tired reply, weighted by the heaviness of resignation.

Shutting her eyes tightly, Vanessa listened to the sound of his footsteps as he walked to the inner door leading to the bedroom and private bath. A broken sigh came from her throat when the door was closed behind him. She opened her eyes wide and took several deep breaths to stop the shaking inside.

There were sounds of Race moving about in the next room, dresser drawers being opened and closed. Too on edge to remain stationary, Vanessa went first to a window, intending to open it and let some fresh air into the stuffy apartment, but it refused to budge.

Frustrated, she turned back to the room, her glance sweeping its contents. She twisted her fingers together, a nervous ball of energy. Waiting gave her too much time to think about the past. And she didn't want to venture over old ground.

Work had always proved to be the best distraction, so she crossed to a water-ringed end table where a black telephone sat. But when she picked up the receiver to dial the shop, the line was dead. Obviously it had been disconnected, even though the phone hadn't been removed. In irritation, Vanessa slammed the receiver onto its cradle.

The none-too-sturdy end table wobbled under the force of it. An empty beer bottle fell onto the floor. Vanessa automatically picked it up, and another one that was sitting near it. She spied a tall wastebasket in the kitchen area and deposited the bottles in it.

From that point, her actions became purely instinct as she gathered up the rest of the beer bottles scattered about the room and emptied the overflowing ashtrays. She stacked all the petroleum trade journals in a pile on the coffee table and threw out the old newspapers.

The shower was running when she picked up the lipstick-laden glass and carried it to the sink. It was the same shade of red lipstick that sexy Marie had been wearing. Vanessa took perverse note of another glass in the sink that had pink lipstick on it. It seemed ridiculous to be glad that Marie had competition.

Leaving the red-stained glass with the other dirty dishes in the sink, she went back to the living area of the room and began picking up the dirty clothes left lying about. A plaid workshirt was draped over the back of the dark green sculptured couch. Vanessa added it to the armful of other clothes before she noticed another article of clothing had been accidentally hidden by the shirt.

For a split second she was paralyzed by a shooting pain that rocked her whole body. Tentatively she reached for the pair of women's nylon panty hose. The instant her fingertips touched the sheer fabric, her nails curled into it like the claws of a cat. She wanted to scream at the top of her lungs, and clamped her teeth tightly shut so she couldn't.

The connecting room from the bedroom swung open, its turning click resounding through the room. Vanessa realized that she couldn't hear the shower running and pivoted as Race entered the apartment's main room.

The springing thickness of his hair had an ebony sheen, curling damply from the shower spray. Its wetness seemed to intensify the dark brown of his eyes and the bronze luster of his tan. Vanessa recognized the gray silk shirt as one that she had bought him for his birthday. It had been one of the last happy occasions they'd had together. Her heart was squeezed by the knowledge that she was standing there with another woman's nylons in her hand.

Race glanced at the pile of dirty clothes in her arm, then made a small sweep of the room, minus its previous clutter. There was a mocking curl to his mouth.

"The proverbial woman's touch," he murmured. "I should have known you couldn't resist it."

"Please don't try to insinuate that other women haven't left their little 'touches' in your apartment." It hurt to speak, the rasping ache making her voice come out husky. "Or maybe you don't classify this as decoration?"

She tossed the tightly wadded ball of ladies' nylons in his direction. They floated to the floor midway between them. Race walked casually over and picked them up, holding them loosely in his hand.

Feeling that she was somehow betraying herself, Vanessa dropped the armload of clothes onto the floor. "The next time Marie pops over to borrow a cup of sugar, you'll have to remember to return them to her," she suggested with fake indifference.

"It might prove awkward, since she insists she's allergic to them. She swears she doesn't own a pair," Race taunted, subtly making it clear that they belonged to someone else.

"You always were very good at remembering little details. It was just the big things you forgot," she flared.

Her hands were clenched into rigid fists at her side as Vanessa trembled with the force of her jealousies. It was a cruel truth. She was insanely jealous of the owner of those nylons, and furious, too, with Race for taunting her with the knowledge that there were many others willing to take her place. She averted her head and stared at the floor, breathing with difficulty. Her peripheral vision warned her of Race's approach.

"I do believe it bothers you to find some other woman's nylons in my apartment," he mused.

"Don't be ridiculous," Vanessa snapped. "I couldn't care less."

His fingers gripped her chin in a punishing hold and forced her to turn her head and look at him. She knew her cheeks were flushed and her eyes were shimmering. He noted both facts with satisfaction.

"Yes, you're jealous," Race stated with a slow nod. "You don't want me, but neither do you want me to have the pleasure of some other woman. That's very selfish of you, Vanessa, but you always were selfish."

"That's not true," she denied.

"You still can't see it, can you?" he murmured cynically. "I'd be gone four or five days, and when I'd come home, all I wanted was to be with you, but you wanted me to take you to some party. It didn't matter what I wanted."

"You always wanted the same thing," she accused.

The corners of his mouth deepened in a smile, but the light in his eyes hardened. "Sex. You still can't say the word, can you?" Race mocked, and deliberately lowered his gaze to her breasts, straining now in agitation against the thin fabric of her blouse. He knew how it disturbed her when he looked at her with such intimate knowledge. "You have an exciting body, Vanessa, but you were always afraid to enjoy it."

"Stop it," she hissed desperately.

"I think I got tired of constantly having to fight all of your inhibitions," he decided, as if he had just reached that conclusion.

"You're implying that I'm frigid—and I'm not," Vanessa protested.

"No, you're not," Race agreed with a mild shake of his head. He let go of her chin to curve his hand along the side of her neck and run his thumb over her jawline. "You can be very passionate—as long as it's the right time and the right place. But if it isn't ten o'clock at night and you aren't in the bedroom, then making love is out of the question as far as you're concerned."

"I wanted to be more than just your sex partner," she insisted in self-defense. "I wanted to be treated as your wife. Marriage is more than a license to make love, but that's all ours was. You weren't interested in a home or a family—"

"Considering the way it turned out, it's a damned good thing we didn't have any kids, isn't it?" Race challenged. "Your memory may be faulty, but mine isn't. As I recall, you were the one who didn't want to have a baby right away."

"That's because we couldn't afford it, Race," Vanessa reminded him.

His mouth thinned. "Which is another way of saying that you didn't trust me to provide for us."

"Could you?" She was stung into retaliating by the contempt in his voice. The glitter of hard amethyst was in the darting glance she gave his apartment. "Is this an example of how you would have provided for us?"

The hand on her neck tightened as he hooked an arm around her waist and yanked her against him with brute force. It stole the wind from her lungs and sent a clamor of alarm through her senses. The length of her body was crushed against his unyielding male form while her head was forced back. The chiseled angles and planes of his face wore the harshness of anger. Vanessa knew she had gone too far, indirectly insulting his manhood, but the things he'd said had hurt her, and she had wanted to strike back. His eyes narrowed dangerously on her face.

"I went through hell with you once," Race muttered on a savage breath. "And I don't give a damn what you think of this place . . . or the women I entertain. And, yes, it's women in the plural. I am a man, although you tried your damnedest to change me into something less."

"I didn't," she whispered, intending to add "not intentionally," but Race didn't give her the chance.

"Like hell you didn't," he snarled, and roughly pushed her away from him, to stand rigidly. "No more," he said thickly. "Never again am I going to let you tie me into knots until I'm nearly crazy."

She numbly moved her head from side to side in a mute denial, but Race didn't take any notice. The tension in the air was so high that Vanessa could almost hear the static crackle of it. Then there was a sudden mocking slant of his mouth.

"I thought I was over you. My God, that's a laugh," he declared with self-derisive amusement.

She knew exactly what he meant, because she couldn't be indifferent to him, either. Theirs had been a relationship of extremes—love or hate. They'd never found a comfortable middle ground where they could coexist. Four years of separation hadn't changed that.

"Race—"

"Shut up, Vanessa." There was a sudden flatness to his voice, as if all emotion had been pulled from it. "We were on our way to the hospital. This conversation isn't going anywhere —unlike our marriage, which had a beginning and an end. So let's get out of here."

"Yes," she agreed, suddenly feeling emotionally drained, too.

There was no sign of Marie when they left his apartment and walked down the hall to the stairs. Jazz music was muffled by her closed door, letting Vanessa know the woman was inside.

It was a strange silence that enveloped them during the drive to the hospital. It was neither comfortable nor strained, as if each of them was alone in a private little space. Vanessa found hers lonely.

A telephone message had been left at the nurses' station for Vanessa, giving her the perfect excuse to let Race see his father privately. She meant to explain to Race that she hadn't told the hospital they were divorced in case they wouldn't allow her to visit Phillip, but it didn't seem appropriate to bring that up now.

She used the telephone in the waiting room to call her secretary, Carla Austin. It took only a few minutes for Carla to inform her of the day's events and pass on the phone calls that had come in for her. Then Vanessa assured Carla that she would be in the shop tomorrow so there wasn't any need to cancel her appointments.

When she hung up the phone, it was hard to believe that all this had happened since this morning. Surely it was longer ago than that. Vanessa felt tired, mentally and physically exhausted. And hungry, she realized. She hadn't eaten anything since breakfast, which had consisted of coffee and croissants. She decided to just look in on Phillip for a minute, then have a bite to eat at the hospital cafeteria before it closed.

Entering the intensive-care unit, Vanessa noticed the oxygen tent was removed and Phillip was breathing on his own. Race had pulled up a straight chair and was sitting by the side of the bed, leaning forward to rest his elbows on his knees. She walked to the opposite side of the bed. Phillip was conscious, his eyes alert and bright as he smiled at her, looking more like his old self. All the tubes and I.V. stands kept her from getting close.

"You seem better," she observed with a relieved smile.

"Having the two of you here, I . . ." The older man choked up. "It's good," he concluded finally. "Race tells me that you personally tracked him down to let him know about me. Thank you."

"It was nothing," Vanessa lied, because she didn't want Phillip to know how her good deed had backfired into another one of their bitter arguments.

With a slight turn of his head, he looked at Race. "Where were you? You never did say."

"Assumption Parish. I'm drilling a well there," Race stated. "We spudded in about three months back, so it won't be long before we reach total depth."

"Why won't you give it up, son?" There was acute sadness in his father's voice. "I have wildcatters coming in and out of my bank every day, millionaires one time and begging for a loan the next. Those oil fields are just going to break your heart."

"We've been through this before, Dad," he responded in a level tone, his glance flicking briefly to Vanessa.

"How much have you got wrapped up in this well, Race?" his father asked with a certain wryness. "A half-million and more probably. You know as well as I do that the odds are nine to one against you. What happens if this one is a 'duster' too?"

"I've acquired a lease on some prime acreage in Livingston Parish and I'm putting the capital together to start drilling there. It's in the Tuscaloosa Sand Trend, one of the hottest plays in the Southeast." That gleam was in his eyes, a reflection of that burning drive that wouldn't let him quit. "If the Boar's Head turns out to be dry or a 'pickle factory,'" Race said, using the petroleum industry's slang term for a well that produces salt water, "or even if it turns out to be a producer, I'll be setting up another drilling operation near Baton Rouge."

"It's always the next well, isn't it?" his father sighed.

"It's the independent oil companies, the wildcatters, that drill nine out of every ten wells in this country, not the majors. For every four barrels of oil taken out of the reserves, we've managed to find three to replace them." Race defended the worth of his profession and the vital role it played. "It's a gamble every time the bit goes in the ground, but it's my choice."

"But there's no future in it," his father insisted, and appealed to Vanessa. "Can't you talk some sense into him, Vanessa? I control the board at the bank. All I have to do is tell them to put Race in charge, and he could take over tomorrow."

She avoided looking at Race as she smiled stiffly at his father. "He didn't listen to me when we were married, so he isn't likely to listen to me now. Why don't you find another subject to talk about besides oil?" Vanessa suggested, because the two would never see eye to eye on it. "There's no need for you to be getting upset, Phillip."

"I know," he sighed heavily. "But he's my son. How can I keep quiet when he is wasting—"

Vanessa lifted a silencing hand. "Change the subject," she advised. "Ask Race about his neighbor. I'm going to the cafeteria and grab a bite to eat."

She could have bitten off her tongue for suggesting that topic the instant she caught the gleam of dry amusement in Race's look, but it was too late. As she made a hasty retreat, she tried to assure herself that it didn't matter. Race had already guessed that she was jealous. Vanessa supposed it was natural, as he had implied, that she resented another woman sharing the intimacies they had once known with each other.

The meal had a reviving effect on her, filling

the emptiness that had contributed to her tiredness. When she returned to Phillip's floor, Race was at the nurses' station, leaning casually on the counter and talking to an attractive blond nurse on duty. She felt his challenging look, but didn't meet it.

When she started to pass him right by to go directly in to see his father, Race fell in step beside her. "Visiting hours are over for tonight," he informed her.

"Oh." She glanced at the slim gold watch on her wrist, slowing her steps. "I didn't think I was gone that long."

He caught her wrist and lifted it to examine the watch, both of them halting in the hospital corridor. "Very nice," he murmured coolly. "And very expensive. Is it a gift from an admirer?"

"I suppose you could say that." She withdrew her wrist from his loose hold, her pulse accelerating at his touch. "Your father gave it to me last Christmas."

"You should have married him instead of me," Race said.

Her breath-filled laugh held little humor. "I've thought about that more than once."

"It's just as well you didn't," he replied. "I could never have handled you being my stepmother."

"What's the difference?" Vanessa retorted. "You couldn't handle me being your wife."

"Which reminds me." Race ignored her jibe. "The hospital staff is under the impression that we are still man and wife. It seems you neglected to mention we are divorced."

"There's a reason for that," she said, unconsciously covering the bareness of her ring finger. "They weren't allowing anyone to see Phillip who wasn't a member of the immediate family. I was afraid they wouldn't let me in, so I omitted telling them."

"Well, they know now." His level gaze studied her quietly. "I wouldn't worry about it. They expect Dad to be taken out of Intensive Care tomorrow and transferred to a private room. So they'll lift the visitor restrictions."

She nodded a brief acknowledgment of the news. "If visiting hours are over, I guess there's no more reason to stay." Vanessa felt her nervousness building under his steady regard. "Do you want me to drop you off at your apartment on my way home?"

"But it isn't on your way home," Race pointed out. "You don't need to bother. I've already got a ride."

"Oh?" Startled by his statement, she blurted her curiosity. "With whom?"

"The blonde on duty." He indicated the young nurse at the station with a nod of his head. "She lives a block from my place."

"You always did work fast." Vanessa bit out the words.

"Connie and I have been out a few times, so this isn't the first time we've met," Race corrected that impression.

"I see." It didn't seem to do any good to insist that she had no right to be jealous. She was. "In that case, there's very little else to say, except good night." She tried to extract herself from the scene as gracefully as she could.

"Good night, Vanessa," Race responded.

As she walked down the corridor, she could feel his gaze following her. Vanessa experienced a little throbbing ache in the region of her heart.

Chapter Four

Vanessa telephoned Phillip at least once during the day and went by the hospital every evening after the shop closed to visit him. In just one short week after his heart attack, he seemed to make remarkable progress, a little of his strength and healthy vigor returning each day.

Only on two occasions did she run into Race at the hospital, and neither time did they exchange more than a few civil comments. From Phillip she had learned Race had gone back to the drilling site three days ago. There had been an ambivalent mixture of relief and regret that it was unlikely she'd be seeing him again.

On Wednesday, everything seemed to go wrong at the shop. There had been a mix-up in the measurements for some special-order drapes.

None of them fit the windows. Naturally Vanessa had a furious client on her hands because she was throwing a big party that weekend and she was going to have bare windows in her living room. Then, her assistant, Peter "Pierre" Benoit, threw an artistic tantrum that had reduced Carla to tears.

Vanessa nearly didn't go to the hospital after she locked the shop doors for the night. But Phillip was expecting her. Knowing that Phillip was becoming bored from nothing to do, she decided to stop by for a few minutes.

As she approached the opened door to his private room, she heard Phillip talking to someone. When her name was mentioned, Vanessa paused to listen.

". . . not knowing from one day to the next if she's going to have a place to eat or sleep," Phillip was saying. "If you'd give up this foolish business and take over for me at the bank, I know you could get her back."

She breathed in sharply, realizing he must be talking to Race. Vanessa held that breath, her guess confirmed in the next second when she heard him reply.

"If I have to give up my business, I don't want her back." It was a hard, flat rejection of the idea, issued without any hesitation. Race hadn't even paused to consider it.

The breath she'd so silently held was released in a deflating sigh. Race couldn't have made his position plainer. She had been cherishing a silent hope that he might be regretting his adamancy at the time of their divorce, and perhaps would have even acted differently if given a second chance. But that wasn't so.

Lost in thought, Vanessa had blocked out most of the activity going on around her. She started visibly when a familiar voice spoke to her, coming from right beside her.

"Hello, Vanessa." Sybil Devereux, Phillip's secretary, sent a warm but harried smile at Vanessa when she turned. "Are you on your way in to see Phillip, or just leaving?"

A small cowardly streak in her wanted to say she was just leaving, but she was bound to be caught in the lie if Sybil mentioned seeing her to Phillip, which was likely. Her mouth was stiff but she forced it to curve in a responding smile.

"On my way in," Vanessa admitted, and took the last two steps to cross the door's threshold to enter Phillip's private room, with Sybil accompanying her.

Race was standing at the window with his back to the door. The sleeves of his white shirt were rolled back, exposing the sinewed strength of tanned forearms. With a turn of his head, he glanced over his shoulder, his expressionless gaze meeting and holding Vanessa's for the span of a second. There was a strong, unnerving flutter of her pulse.

"Hello, Phillip." Vanessa quickly redirected her attention to the man in the bed, wearing a conservative maroon robe. "How are you feeling?"

"Fine. Fine." He repeated himself in an automatic reply to a question he'd heard much too often. His gaze went past Vanessa to the older woman with her. "Sybil. I was wondering what time you'd arrive. Did you and Vanessa come together?"

"No, we met outside in the hallway," Vanessa replied, conscious that Race had turned from the window and was watching her. "Hello, Race." She looked at him, fighting the little ache in her throat. "I didn't expect to find you here. I thought you'd gone back to your well."

"I did, but I had to come back to New Orleans on business, so I decided to check and see how Dad was doing." His gaze traveled over her length, making an absent inspection of the cool seersucker suit she was wearing—white with a thin navy stripe over a gauzy navy blouse. The outfit created a very poised and professional look rather than flattering.

"I see," she murmured, unable to think of anything suitably casual to say to continue the conversation.

"How are things at the bank, Sybil?" Phillip inquired with the keenness of a man anxious to get back to his work.

"It's running smoothly," she answered, but he didn't look pleased by the assurance.

"Now, that is a lie, Sybil." He pointed a scolding finger at her. "It never runs smoothly."

"All right," his secretary conceded with a smile. "There've been a few rocky patches, but nothing we couldn't handle."

The number of visitors in Phillip's room swelled from three to five as two executive officers of his bank entered. It was more than the room could comfortably accommodate. Tension threaded stiffly through her limbs when Vanessa realized Race was at her side. Her darted glance was held by the probing quality of his steady gaze.

"Let's get out of here and I'll buy you a cup of coffee," he suggested in a low voice meant only for her hearing.

The invitation took her by surprise. Vanessa heard herself agreeing without taking a moment to consider the wisdom of it. Not by any stretch of the imagination could it be said that they were on friendly terms. Yet Vanessa found the idea appealing.

Even if she had wanted to, she wasn't given a chance to change her mind. Race interrupted his father's conversation with the two bank members long enough to inform him they were leaving, then ushered Vanessa out of the room.

The guiding touch of the hand on the back of her waist was unsettling in a familiar way. It seemed to take away all her hostility, all the animosity Race usually aroused in her, and replaced it with something warm and tremulous. Vanessa had no idea what she could discuss with him, but she knew she didn't want to argue with him this time.

At the hospital cafeteria, they skipped the food line and went directly to the end where the drinks were. Race set two cups of hot coffee on a tray and pushed it to the cash register. Vanessa wasn't intentionally trying to snoop when she watched him take his billfold from a hip pocket to pay for the coffee, but she couldn't help noticing all he had in his wallet were four one-dollar bills. He spent one of them paying for the coffee. It preyed on her mind to know how short of cash he was.

After slipping the change into his pocket, Race picked up the tray. "There's an empty table by the wall. Is that all right?"

"It's fine," she agreed absently, and followed when Race led the way to it.

Once they were seated, the silence lengthened. Vanessa curved both hands around her cup, the heat from the coffee burning into her palms. It was impossible not to be conscious of the strong, sun-browned hands across the narrow table from her, or their male owner. She searched for some safe question to open the conversation.

"How did you get here?" she finally asked. "Did you drive?"

"Yes." His mouth quirked briefly, drawing her gaze to its male shape. "So I'm not trying to cadge a ride."

"It didn't occur to me that you might be," Vanessa replied, feeling they had started out on the wrong foot already. She lifted her cup, glancing at him over its rim, and tried a different subject. "How is the drilling going?"

"It's coming along fine." His craggy features wore a dryly amused look. "It isn't necessary to pretend to be interested in my progress—or lack of it, Vanessa."

"I'm not pretending," she denied, and felt uncomfortable with the lie, because her interest was only superficial. She knew nothing about the problems or procedures in drilling for oil or natural gas.

"This is a first, then," Race said, and lifted his coffeecup in a mocking toast to the occasion. "When we were married, I had the distinct impression that you only asked about my work because you were secretly hoping I'd fail. Admit it, Vanessa, you were glad when the wells came in dry."

"I wasn't." But she remembered feeling smugly complacent because she had told-him-so. Looking back, she could see how she had rubbed it in.

There was a brief shake of his dark head to reject her automatic denial. "Even that last well"—his voice was level and subdued, recounting facts without any cynical or bitter overtones—"when I lost every dime I had, you weren't angry because we lost the house. You thought for sure I was going to accept a vice-presidency in Dad's bank. That's what you wanted me to do. When you found out I was putting another investment together to drill a new well, that's when you walked out and filed for a divorce.

"Yes." She admitted it, her chin lifting at a slightly defiant angle. "When I realized you hadn't learned your lesson from that, there didn't seem to be any point in going on. If you were so irresponsible as to risk our home and our marriage, then they obviously didn't mean very much to you." A surge of agitation swept through her as Vanessa abruptly set her cup on the table and clenched it tightly. "It's all in the past now, Race. Do we have to keep raking it up? Can't we just . . . talk?"

"About what?" he challenged with cynical lightness. "Was there ever a subject we agreed on?"

A raw tension licked along her nerve ends, but she determinedly ignored his taunt. "Did Phillip happen to mention to you that the doctor said they would probably be sending him home next week?"

"Yes, he told me." Race mocked her choice of subjects, since it was so short-lived, ending with his answer.

"It's futile, isn't it?" She searched his sun-hardened features with a kind of resigned sadness. "We can't talk about anything without sniping at each other, can we?"

Race took a drink of his coffee and didn't comment on her observation. "What's been happening in your life these past four years? Dad said something about you starting your own business. An interior-decorating shop, right?"

"Yes." Vanessa didn't elaborate, doubting that Race really cared.

"You always had a knack for that, I remember," he said. "You were talking about getting into that when we met, weren't you?"

"Yes. That's why I was working for that furniture store, so I could get some practical experience before applying at a professional shop."

"What made you decide to strike out on your own instead of going to work for someone else?" he asked curiously.

"At the time, there weren't any openings." Vanessa went on to explain how his father had encouraged her into setting up her own shop when she wasn't able to find a position with any of the decorating firms in the metropolitan area.

Her cup was empty before she realized how adeptly Race had manipulated the conversation until she had told him all about her initial trials of getting started and the subsequent success she had achieved. Even her social life had entered into the conversation, since a great many of her contacts had been made that way.

"Haven't you found yourself a steady, reliable guy who can offer the security you think is so important?" Race mocked, but with a gentle smile.

"Not yet." Vanessa shrugged the answer. But his description of "steady and reliable" fit several of the men she had dated. It was a little startling to remember how dull they had been, but she didn't mention that. Someone walked by with a plateful of food. The aroma of fried chicken wafted past Vanessa, reminding her how long it had been since lunch. "Have you eaten yet?" she asked Race.

His split-second hesitation prompted her to recall how short of funds he was. "No." It was a clipped answer.

On impulse she suggested, "Let's have dinner together. We can go to that little seafood restaurant out by Lake Pontchartrain." She could see the refusal forming in his expression, so she hastened to add, "It'll be my treat."

A muscle flexed along his jawline. "No thanks."

"Why not?" Vanessa argued lightly. "You paid for my coffee. Why can't I buy your dinner?"

"Dinner is a bit more expensive than coffee," he reminded her with a stiff smile.

"What difference does that make?" she persisted, and guessed it was his pride that was making him turn down her invitation because he couldn't afford to buy her dinner. "You accepted a ride to New Orleans with me, and I paid for the gasoline."

"But you were making the drive whether I rode with you or not." It was a minor point but a very significant one as far as Race was concerned.

Irritated by the feeling that she had come up against an immovable object, Vanessa tried another approach. "All right. If you won't let me buy you dinner, then why don't you come to my apartment and I'll fix us something to eat?"

For a long second he considered her with a lazily disguised closeness. "On one condition."

"What's that?" She lifted her head, wondering what it could be.

"That I'll stop by a grocery store on the way to your place and buy the food."

There was impatience in the laughing breath she expelled. "That's ridiculous. I have ham steaks and fresh shrimp for cocktails in my refrigerator," Vanessa protested. "There's no need for you to buy any food."

"Let's get this straight, Vanessa." A hard light

glittered in his dark eyes. "It's going to be a cold day in hell when I let you pay for the food I eat. And I don't give a damn how broke or hungry I am."

"You're overly sensitive," she snapped, impatient with him for making her invitation sound like charity.

"If I am, it's thanks to you." He placed both hands on the table to shove his chair back. "I'll meet you at your apartment in half an hour."

"Do you have the address?" she asked, standing up to leave.

"Yes." But he didn't say how he had obtained it. It was hardly a secret, since she was listed in the phone book. Phillip could have given it to him, for that matter. There was a small run of pleasure that Race had taken the time to find out where she lived.

In the hospital parking lot, they separated. As Vanessa drove her Porsche onto the street, she noticed the mud-spattered tan pickup truck reversing out of its stall. It was too far away to read the black lettering on the door panel, but she recognized the snarling wildcat decal below it.

Her apartment was located in the block of buildings fronting Jackson Square in the very heart of the New Orleans French Quarter. It had taken her over a year to fix it just the way she wanted it, but the warm, cozy atmosphere she had managed to create partially compensated for the fact that she lived alone.

Arriving ahead of Race, Vanessa took advantage of that to quickly straighten up. She took off her light suit jacket and hung it in the closet.

There wasn't time to change out of her pencil-slim skirt and navy blouse, but she did freshen her makeup and add a few more pins to keep the French coil hairstyle looking neat.

As she left the bedroom, there was a knock at her door. Vanessa paused and pressed a hand against the sudden tightening of her stomach. Her lips felt dry despite the coating of gloss she'd just applied. She moistened them and walked to the door.

When she opened the door to admit Race, she couldn't think of a casual greeting. He said nothing either as he stepped inside. His gaze skimmed over her see-through blouse, taking note of the lacy outline of her navy-blue bra. He carried a small grocery sack in the crook of his arm.

"I'll take that into the kitchen," Vanessa murmured nervously, and reached for the paper bag.

Race handed it to her and let his gaze travel around the apartment. "Very fashionable—comfortable and quietly elegant," he observed, letting his attention return to her. A faintly caustic note entered his voice. "What else would one expect from the home of an interior decorator, hmm?"

"I like it." It was a defensive answer, pricked by the insinuation that he didn't.

His heavy sigh was laced with grimness. "Sorry," he said curtly. "It is nice."

But she couldn't take much pleasure from such a grudging admission. "I'll get dinner started." She moved toward the small kitchen, carrying the grocery sack.

Race followed her, and leaned a shoulder against the archway. Vanessa was proud of the way she had decorated it. Butcher-block countertops and varying sizes of copper pans hanging above the stove gave it a homey touch, she thought, but she doubted Race would see it that way. And she wasn't about to ask.

She set the sack down on the counter and opened the top to see what he'd bought. There was a bag of English muffins, a carton of eggs, and some wrapped meat.

"I remembered that you used to be good at fixing eggs Benedict," Race said. "I hope you haven't lost your touch."

"It's been a while, but I don't think so." She unwrapped the Canadian bacon and set it to one side. For a short while after they were first married, it had become almost a ritual Sunday-morning breakfast. The dish had been part of some of their happier times before all the trouble had started.

"It wasn't all bad between us," Race murmured, as if following the direction of her thoughts.

"No, not all bad," Vanessa agreed tightly, then forced a smile. "Why don't you go watch television while I cook dinner?"

"Are you trying to say I'm not any help?" There was a dancing glint in his eyes, ignoring the elemental tension that charged the air between them.

"Something like that," she retorted, trying to match his mood.

Race smiled lazily and disappeared into the

living room. A few seconds later she heard the sound of a television program. It was impossible to forget he was in the next room. All the while she was frying the bacon and whipping up the hollandaise sauce, the thought kept hammering at her mind that she had made a mistake inviting Race to her apartment. She was starting to forget all the reasons their marriage hadn't worked and starting to remember the physical side of their relationship.

His masculinity was a potent force, his rugged good looks too disturbing. In those first few weeks of marriage, Race had so easily broken down her barriers of modesty. It had taken a long time to rebuild them. He had been so casual about nudity and sex, constantly teasing her for being so uptight about both. But he hadn't understood her need for security, either.

The dining room occupied a small niche off the kitchen, with a narrow table positioned in front of the window overlooking Jackson Square. There was an unobstructed view of the sidewalk artists exhibiting their paintings on the ornate iron fence around the square, and the picturesque horses and carriages that took tourists on rides through the French Quarter.

Vanessa arranged the place settings for two and tried not to remember this was the first time she had entertained any man other than Race's father in her apartment. She waited until she had carried the plates to the table, a garnish of parsley sprigs adding color to the golden sauce covering the poached eggs and bacon-topped muffins; then she called to Race.

"Would you like milk to drink, or coffee later?" she inquired when he came to the table.

"Coffee later," he said, pulling out a chair to sit down. "It looks good."

"Thank you." Vanessa smoothed the paisley napkin over her lap.

"How long has it been since we've sat across the table from each other?" Race mused.

"A long time." The muscles in her throat constricted. She had trouble swallowing the first bite. The conversation was not taking a safe course, so she changed it. "I've always wondered, Race, why you've stayed in the oil business. Why you keep trying, when you haven't managed to hit anything in all these years."

"That's not entirely true," he corrected. "I've got a half-dozen 'stripper' wells producing. They bring in enough to take care of my office overhead."

"'Stripper' wells?" Most of the slang terms were foreign to her. She wondered why she hadn't picked up his vernacular during their married years, then realized she hadn't wanted to know.

"It's a gas well that produces under sixty thousand cubic feet of gas a day. A big company wouldn't find it economical to recover that low volume, but I'm not a big company yet."

"What would they do with it?" She frowned.

"Probably flare it—burn it off." Race automatically explained the term, a slight keenness in his expression.

"Is that why you're still in it? Because you've

found a little?" She wondered if the small find was like a carrot being dangled in front of him.

He seemed to consider the question before answering it. "It's the challenge. Like a mountain you climb because it's there. In this case, it's the challenge of discovering it."

"And once you discover it?" Vanessa prompted, trying to understand his apparent compulsion.

"There's always more out there waiting to be found," he reminded her. "When you decorate someone's home, do you quit? Isn't there always another house, another room, that challenges your ability?"

"Yes," she conceded the point. "But not with the risks—financial risks you take."

"It's only money." His shoulders lifted in an expressive shrug of indifference.

"That's because you don't look past today. You're thirty-six years old—in your prime. You can laugh at security. But what happens when you're seventy-two and you're broke?" Vanessa argued. "You have to provide for that eventuality. If you're always gambling everything you own, how can you ever have security in your later years?"

"It's simple." The corners of his mouth twitched. "I'm never going to get old."

"How can you joke about it?" she declared in irritation.

"Because I don't want to argue with you," Race stated. "It's bad for the digestion. I don't want to ruin a good meal."

"That's so typical of you." An anger born out of frustration brought smarting tears to her eyes. Vanessa bent her head to hide them and stabbed a fork at her food. "You never would discuss it. That was your life and that was the way it was going to be. Your attitude always was: I could take it or leave it. It didn't matter what I wanted. You wouldn't even talk about it."

"And today we are divorced." There was a harshness in his voice, assertive and blunt. "So it shouldn't matter in my old age. You go ahead and live your life the way you want to, and let me worry about mine."

"Which is another way of avoiding the issue," she murmured bitterly. The food seemed suddenly tasteless, its flavor departing along with her appetite.

"Why don't we agree to differ?" Race challenged.

The air was so thick with bared hostility that Vanessa could hardly breathe. Her stomach was churning from the emotional turmoil that buffeted her. This was not the way she had wanted it—this was never the way she had wanted it.

"This always happens, doesn't it?" She lifted her gaze from the plate to look at him. There was stormy confusion in her violet eyes. "If we're together more than five minutes, we're at each other's throats."

Race didn't deny it. "We both have scars that haven't healed—and we know just what to say to hurt the other person."

"But why?" Vanessa demanded in taut bewilderment. "I put all that bitterness and resentment behind me. I have a career and a beautiful apartment. Our marriage is over and done with, so why can't we at least be civil to each other?"

"Maybe because it isn't over and done with between us," Race suggested while his dark gaze traveled from her eyes to her mouth and back again. "Maybe the ashes have been smoldering for the past four years. You've got to admit the heat is still there. A little fanning, and we'd have a fire."

"No." She wouldn't accept that possibility. She had lived in that inferno once. Only a fool would brave the flames a second time. "Excuse me." Vanessa laid her napkin alongside her plate and pushed her chair away from the table. "I think I'll check on the coffee."

Chapter Five

Coffee was just an excuse Vanessa used to escape his disturbing presence and the volatility that always surrounded them when they were together. She stopped in front of the glass coffee-maker and gripped the edge of the counter, shaken by a violent shudder.

There was a seething conflict of emotions raging inside her. Bitterness, resentment, and pain were all tearing at her. It didn't make any sense that she was letting Race affect her this way. What kind of invisible hold did he have on her? Why hadn't she left well enough alone and stayed away from him? Instead, she had invited him here—to her apartment for dinner. Out of pity? How could she feel sorry for someone who ripped her heart to pieces?

A footstep sounded on the tiled floor behind her, warning Vanessa that she was no longer alone in the kitchen. There was a burning sensation that traveled from the back of her neck down the curving length of her spine, the path his inspecting gaze was taking. It radiated through her nervous system in a rippling effect that sensitized all her nerve ends to his presence.

Vanessa quickly made herself busy, opening the cupboard door above the coffeemaker and taking down two cups. "The coffee is finished." Despite her attempt at indifferent briskness, there was a betraying quiver in her voice. "Shall I pour it now?"

His hands moved onto her shoulder bones, and Vanessa stiffened at the contact that was both familiar and disturbing. The warmth from his body shimmered over her like heat waves, distorting the distance that remained between them and minimizing it until he seemed closer.

"Forget the coffee," Race instructed in a thick, low voice that vibrated through her. "Haven't you guessed yet why we've been arguing ever since we met again?"

"No." It was a small sound as Vanessa held herself motionless, her breath running shallow while her pulse hammered wildly in her throat. She was afraid the least movement might act as an explosive catalyst.

"Because we were both trying to avoid this." There was a slow, exploring slide of his hands downward to the soft flesh of her upper arms, as if he was rediscovering the way she felt. "As long as we were fighting, we could keep a safe distance between us. But if we stopped, we might find out we still wanted each other."

His hands exerted a slight pressure to draw her a few inches backward. Her lips parted in protest, but no sound came out. At the stirring touch of his breath on her hair, Vanessa closed her eyes in a weak attempt to block out his existence. But she only succeeded in heightening her other senses.

The sharp, stimulating fragrance of his aftershave became stronger, its heady scent working on her mute resistance. Lifting her chin high, Vanessa tried turning her head away in hopes of eluding his strongly male smell. But she had unwittingly left herself open to a more tangible assault on her defenses.

She didn't realize her error until she felt the tantalizing brush of his mouth on the long curve of her neck. She tensed for a rigid instant, then melted at the searing enjoyment of his nibbling caress.

With a half-smothered groan, Race circled his arms around the front of her waist and gathered her against him. The whole length of her body was heated by the contact with his hard, male outline from the solid columns of his thighs and the angular thrust of his hips to the dominating breadth of his muscled chest.

"I want you, Vanessa," he muttered thickly. His mouth moved roughly near her ear, its moistness tangling her hair and messing its smooth style. "I've never stopped wanting you, although God knows I've tried."

"No." She didn't want to hear that. It was too seductive, and she didn't want to get caught in the undertow of his desire, but there was a sinking feeling that it was already too late.

His hands glided upward to cup the undersides of her breasts as they strained against the confinement of her thin clothes. There was an aching familiarity to his intimate caress, so arousing and possessive. It was difficult to remember that Race had no right to touch her like this—with such ease.

"You want me, too. I can feel the way you're trembling." His hold tightened to fit her more closely to his muscled length and absorb the little shudders of reluctant longing.

"But I don't." Not with her mind, because Vanessa knew Race would only break her heart again. But her body didn't care. She resented his sexual skill that could arouse her desire until it took precedence over her will.

"Why do you always have to deny it?" he demanded roughly, a biting impatience in his voice. "Why can't you be honest about your feelings and desires? There's no shame in passion. Love isn't a dirty four-letter word."

"I never aroused your love," Vanessa protested with an aching throb in her voice. "Only your lust. Anyone would do. You proved that with the number of women you've known since we broke up."

With forceful pressure he turned her around and spread his hand over the side of her face, running his thumb over her lips to familiarize himself with their soft curves. The dark intensity of his gaze seemed to make her heart turn over.

"None of them were you, Vanessa," Race insisted. "They weren't even good imitations. Why do you think I went through so many of them? I kept telling myself there would be another woman out there who could make me feel the way you do. There isn't. I spent four years of searching, so I ought to know."

Beaten by the stroking caress of his thumb that parted her lips, Vanessa swayed against him. With a muffled moan of exulting triumph, he crushed her pliant body to his and combed his fingers into her mink-brown hair, destroying its sleek style and cupping the back of her head in his hand.

He kissed her with a deep, raw hunger that flamed through her blood. His heart thudded wildly beneath her splayed fingers, only a drumbeat faster than her own. She was helpless to combat the fires he started. All she could manage was to keep them under loose control.

His hand moved restlessly up and down her spine. She was virtually breathless when the long kiss ended, but her eyes remained closed as he rubbed his mouth over her face, filling himself with the taste of her.

"I want to go on holding you and kissing you, Vanessa." The heat of his moist breath fanned her already flushed skin. "I want to have you naked in my arms again, your body against mine."

She felt his fingers on her blouse front, searching for the small navy-blue buttons. He wasn't asking if it was what she wanted. Like always, Race didn't care about her wants and needs as long as he was satisfied. Tomorrow didn't mean anything to him, but Vanessa knew if she slept with him tonight, she'd regret it in the morning.

"No." Her first refusal held no conviction, but it gained strength when Vanessa repeated it the second time, more forcefully. "No!" She flattened her hands against his chest and pushed away.

Her sudden use of physical resistance caught him off guard. She was taking a step backward out of his arms before Race could check her escape. For a stunned second his hands remained lifted, reaching out to her. His gaze darkened to black as he watched her fumbling to fasten the one button he had succeeded in freeing.

"What the hell is it this time?" Race demanded in a rumbling growl.

"I don't want you to touch me again." Vanessa braved the dangerous gleam in his eyes and steadily faced him, wary and trembling inwardly with a lusting ache for the very thing she was denying herself.

"It's the wrong room, isn't it?" His glance sliced out to take note of their surroundings, while his upper lip curled with the angry taunt.

"Leave me alone." It was almost a warning, even though she knew she was no match for him physically.

Race moved so quickly for a man his size. One minute there was more than three feet separating them, and in the next, his hand snared her wrist. He ignored her startled outcry of alarm and turned around, dragging her after him as he strode out of the kitchen. No amount of pulling, twisting, or prying succeeded in loosening his iron grip. Her panic mounted when Vanessa realized he was headed for the bedroom.

There was only one window in the room. With dusk settling over the Crescent City, little light streamed through the glass to alleviate the interior dimness. But there was enough to show the location of the bed with its chocolate-and-gold velvet bedspread.

Race stopped a few feet inside the room, but his hand continued to pull on her wrist, using her impetus to impel her forward in a slingshot effect toward the bed. Off balance, Vanessa had to grab a wooden poster to keep from falling onto the mattress. It was an instinctive move that made her try to hide behind the carved mahogany bedpost, as if it could somehow protect her from Race.

He stood in the middle of the room, glaring at her, his feet slightly apart and his hands resting belligerently on his hips. A taut violence seemed to possess him.

"Now what's your excuse?" he hurled savagely. "I suppose it's not dark enough for you!"

In three long strides Race was at the window to yank the shade down and throw the room into almost total darkness. The silence that followed seemed to grip Vanessa by the throat. If it wasn't for the whiteness of his shirt, she wouldn't have been sure of his position.

"When you walked out on me"—his low, harsh voice traveled across the room to cut into her—"at a time when I needed you most, I swore I'd never let you tear me up like that again. I went through hell when you left me. You aren't worth it." His condemnation tore at her, but she managed to choke back the sobs and keep silent. When she saw him move, Vanessa shrank behind the post, trying to make herself small. "This time," Race continued in a cold, contemptuous tone, "I'm the one who's walking out the door. I don't want to be in your bed."

Vanessa heard the sound of his footsteps, but a part of her didn't believe he actually intended to leave. When his lean bulk blocked out the light from the doorway, she stared in frozen silence. Without a backward glance, he disappeared into the living room. Seconds later she heard the slam of the apartment door. Race had left.

Numbly she sank onto the velvet-covered mattress. A tremor started in her legs and traveled all the way up her body. Something wet trickled onto her lips. She licked at it with her tongue and tasted the saltiness of a tear. More followed.

In the three weeks that followed, Vanessa felt like she was living in a vacuum. Nothing seemed to touch her. She went through the motions of doing all the usual things, putting in her regular time at the shop and attending the social functions that might be beneficial to her business, but her heart wasn't in it. She was subdued and quiet, unwilling to reason with clients when she disapproved of their choices of color or fabric.

Phillip Cantrell had been released from the hospital a little over two weeks ago, so her evening visits with him had stopped. Still she called him regularly every day. When he invited her out to dinner on Friday evening, Vanessa accepted without interest.

At seven-thirty on the dot, she drove her silver Porsche up to the entrance to the Pontchartrain Hotel and left it with the doorman to park. As she entered the marble-walled foyer, the heels of her gold shoes made tap-tapping sounds on the tiled floor. She was well aware of the old, elegant hotel's reputation for gourmet cuisine in the Creole tradition.

Her steps faltered as she was jolted by the memory of the first time she had dined here. Race had brought her. She remembered how impressed she had been with the Old World grace and charm of the place. She had gone on and on about the little touches of class that elevated it above other fine hotels. Race had reacted with amusement, that irritating dry and mocking kind.

Vanessa glanced around the foyer with its richly marbled walls. Her cheeks grew warm as she recalled how Race had insisted that she take a closer look at some of the natural designs in the stone's swirling colors. After he had pointed out the second small nude figure in the marble, she had become embarrassed and indignant. She had stiffly informed him that he was crude and vulgar for noticing such things. Race had retaliated by accusing her of being self-righteous and puritanical.

Straying from her course to the hotel's main dining room, Vanessa wandered over by the elevators to study the design in the marble. With the tips of her fingers, she absently traced the outline of a nude. Why wasn't she offended by the sight of it now? Did her acceptance of it come from the accumulation of experience and exposure to a freer discussion of sex by the people she'd met? She had been young and immature when she was Race's wife. She hadn't come to terms with her own sexuality. Did she understand it any better now? Did she accept it?

With a heavy sigh, she turned from the wall and crossed to the short flight of steps that led past the desk to the dining room. The maître d' greeted her with a slight bow and a softly murmured "Good evening."

"Good evening," she responded automatically. "Mr. Phillip Cantrell's table, please."

"He's waiting for you, Mrs. Cantrell," he informed her, then turned with another bowing gesture. "This way, please."

The voices of the fashionably dressed diners at the tables were muted, influenced by the elegant atmosphere that subtly demanded a proper decorum. A cordon of waiters went quietly about their work, trying to attain a kind of invisibility. Even the tinkling splash of water spilling over a decorative fountain could be heard.

When Phillip noticed her approach, he rose from his chair. A faint smile touched her mouth at how healthy he looked. It seemed hard to believe he was recovering from a heart attack. The silvering at his temples had invaded more of his dark hair, but he looked the same otherwise.

"You look wonderful." Vanessa brushed his smoothly shaved cheek with a kiss of greeting before sitting in the chair the maître d' held for her.

"I feel wonderful," Phillip replied. "But I must warn you, if I'm not home by ten o'clock, my car will turn into a pumpkin. It's one of Dr. Foley's curses. And I thought I was too old for a curfew."

Their initial conversation centered around the usual inconsequential chitchat, frequently interrupted by a hovering waiter who offered suggestions on the wine list, went through the ritual of serving it, left the dinner menus, and came back for their order. Vanessa actually did very little of the talking, nodding in all the right places and murmuring an appropriate response when it was necessary.

Phillip lifted his wineglass in a toast. "To my first evening on the town and the lovely lady who is with me."

After a demure nod of her head, Vanessa sipped at the delicate white wine. "Are you certain the doctor allows you to drink alcohol?" she questioned.

"He has restricted me to one glass," Phillip admitted with a rueful smile. "So you'll have to drink this whole bottle by yourself."

"I think not," she murmured.

The appetizer was followed by the main course, fresh red snapper drowning in a spicy

Creole sauce rich with shrimp and crabmeat. Lately, food had been one of the least interesting things in her life but Vanessa found herself enjoying this delectable seafood dish.

"If I have chest pains tonight, I shall never know whether it's indigestion or another heart attack," Phillip declared as he savored each bite with exaggerated pleasure.

"I wish you wouldn't joke about that," Vanessa protested mildly, drawing a keen look from her former father-in-law.

"What's the matter, Vanessa?" He studied her closely, no longer wearing his jovial expression. "You don't seem like yourself tonight. You're unnaturally quiet."

"All I need is a little more wine." But her smile was faint as she took another sip from her wineglass.

"No." He shook his head. "Something's bothering you. How is the decorating business?"

"It couldn't be better," Vanessa replied truthfully.

"Then what is it? Are you tired? Have you been working too hard?" The slight lift of one corner of his mouth reminded Vanessa of Race. She quickly lowered her gaze to her plate.

"I suppose I am a little tired." She pretended that was the reason for her quiet mood, when it was much more complicated than that. "It's the end of a long week."

"You should make a point of resting up over the weekend," he said.

"I will." She stirred her fork idly around in the Creole sauce, struggling to appear offhand as she inquired, "Have you seen anything of Race lately?"

Phillip slowly lowered his fork to the plate while he considered her thoughtfully. "He stopped at the house for an hour shortly after I came home from the hospital. And I talked to him on the telephone just yesterday."

"Oh?" It was a prompting sound. She waited for him to tell her more.

"I've never put much stock in that old cliché about a silver lining behind every cloud, but I guess something good did come out of my heart attack," he said. "It forced you and Race to see each other again. There was a time, not too long ago, when his name didn't enter any of our conversations. I'm glad you can finally talk about him, Vanessa, without any rancor."

"I don't expect we can ever be friends." It was something she regretted. There was a trace of irony in her smile, because their relationship had touched nearly every base but that one—from stranger to lover to mate to enemy. Yet they had never been friends.

"Divorced couples can rarely make that transition," Phillip agreed.

"No, I don't suppose they can." But Vanessa didn't want to talk about that. "How is Race doing? Did he say?"

"Fine." He nodded an affirmative but noninformative answer. "He mentioned that they had drilled to 'total depth' at his well in Assumption Parish. The initial tests showed the presence of natural gas."

Vanessa brightened at the news, a sparkle showing in her violet irises. "That's wonderful."

"It's a little early to say how wonderful," Phillip cautioned wryly. "Race still has to run more tests to see if it's present in sufficient quantity to make it economical to complete the well."

"But just the fact that it's there is a good sign, isn't it?" Vanessa frowned, realizing more of her ignorance about Race's work.

"The odds are against him." The conservative banker in him showed his skepticism for long shots.

"But . . ." She paused, trying to recall the scant statistics she knew. "Didn't you say that the odds were nine to one that he wouldn't find any oil or gas? There is natural gas present, so wouldn't it mean—?"

Phillip was already shaking his head before she could finish the question. "The odds against finding an oil field with a million barrels of recoverable oil—or the equivalent in natural gas—are fifty to one. So the fact that he found natural gas doesn't mean a whole lot."

"I see," she murmured. "How long before he knows?"

"A couple of weeks . . . a month, maybe longer. It depends on a lot of variables." He sighed, the corners of his mouth pulling down. "There was a wildcatter up in Canada that discovered a gas field that could have supplied an entire city the size of Winnipeg. The problem was, it was a kind of gas that wouldn't burn. I've never been able to figure out whether a wildcatter is a special breed of man . . . or just a fool."

"I think . . . they're a special breed," Vanessa hesitantly ventured her opinion.

"You could be right." He smiled at her, briefly sharing a mutual reevaluation of Race.

A small silence ran between them. Vanessa bit at her lower lip, nibbling on it while she debated whether to confide in Phillip about the belated surfacing of doubts that was plaguing her.

"Phillip," she began, hesitating a little, "do you think I was wrong to leave Race?"

He breathed in deeply, surprised by her question. "I can't answer that for you," he denied.

"I'm only asking your opinion," Vanessa reasoned.

"There is very little to be gained by second-guessing," Phillip countered.

"I know . . . but at the time, I was so positive I was doing the right thing. Now, I'm not sure," she admitted.

"My dear." He reached across the table and covered her hand. "No one could say that you didn't have cause to divorce him. It's a man's obligation to provide for his family's future. In Race's business, it's practically impossible—as time has shown. It was unfair of him to ask you to scrimp and save and go without while he literally gambled away everything the two of you owned."

"I know all that." It wasn't the issue that was bothering her. "But he lost everything too. My marriage vow was 'for better or worse.' But when it got worse, I left. I'm beginning to feel like the rat that deserted the sinking ship while the noble captain went down with it."

"Vanessa, you've come to be like my own daughter." Phillip squeezed her hand in deep affection. "I'm not just saying that, either. You are as much a part of my family as Race is. But you are more like me than my own son. I couldn't take the strain and pressure of his kind of life—never knowing from one day to the next whether I'm going to have a dollar in my pocket and a place to sleep. Neither can you."

"But did I try?" Vanessa persisted, unable to shake the guilt she was experiencing.

"From my point of view, you did." He arched an eyebrow. "Are you going to tell me what brought all this on? Was it seeing my son again?"

"Partly," she admitted. "But it was something he said, too."

"What was that?" he asked calmly.

"He accused me of being glad that the well had come in dry and that we'd lost everything."

"That's nonsense," Phillip scoffed at the thought, releasing her hand and leaning back in his chair.

"But it isn't." She lifted her head to look at him. "I was glad, because I thought he'd finally quit that stupid business and go to work for you at the bank. When he didn't, that's when I walked out. I thought if he really loved me, he'd give it up."

"Vanessa, I don't think you're being fair to yourself," he argued reasonably. "If you and

Race were still married today, do you honestly believe things would be any different than they were?"

"Probably not," she sighed, because Race still didn't understand her concern about tomorrow. There was a hint of bitterness in her brief smile. "But I'll never know, will I?"

"Financial problems have broken up more marriages than adultery," Phillip stated. "Yours is definitely not the first." He deliberately changed the subject. "I hope you're going to leave room for dessert. They serve the best mile-high pie in town."

Chapter Six

Outside the French windows of the shop, the shadows in the courtyard were lengthening to indicate the lateness of the afternoon hour. It looked very cool and peaceful to a harassed Vanessa while she tried not to let her true feelings show to her client.

"This isn't what I had in mind at all." Mrs. Perez discarded the two wall-fabric samples Vanessa had selected as being totally unsuitable. "Don't you have something else?"

"Of course." She smiled sweetly.

In her opinion, either of the two choices would have been perfect. Mrs. Perez was being unreasonably picky, Vanessa thought angrily. The woman was redecorating her entire fourteen-room house, and the last two and a half hours had been spent discussing one bathroom. The older woman had very definite ideas about what she wanted. At least that's what Vanessa kept telling herself so she wouldn't lose her temper.

"I want something very dramatic," Mrs. Perez reiterated with a haughty lilt to her voice, betraying her impatience with the time spent.

Vanessa ran the tip of her tongue along her back teeth and silently counted to ten. "Salmon pink and black would make a very striking combination," she suggested with quiet desperation, because it would mean throwing out the few decisions already reached.

The blue-haired woman blinked at her and touched the gleaming strands of pearls around her neck. Slowly a pleased expression stole across her heavily made-up face.

"Black marble with faint swirls of pink through it." Mrs. Perez elaborated on the thought as if visualizing it in her mind's eye. "It would be effective."

"I can assure you there would be nothing else like it in New Orleans," Vanessa murmured, and lifted a hand to signal Carla to come over.

Her secretary doubled as a kind of waitress when they entertained clients in the shop. In her self-effacing way, Carla seemed to materialize beside the sofa, and hovered there like a shy brown moth, awaiting Vanessa's request.

"Mrs. Perez would like to look at the sample marble squares. And would you bring some more coffee, too?" Vanessa indicated the delicate china coffeepot sitting on a tray with two demitasses. The session promised to take longer than Vanessa had realized. She felt in need of the caffeine stimulant so prevalent in the black New Orleans coffee.

As Carla came around the sofa to pick up the coffeepot, the door to the shop opened. Aware that Carla would deal with the customer, Vanessa cast a barely interested glance to see who it was. A tall, dark-haired man had entered the shop, wearing a dark suit and tie.

The shock of disbelief rolled through her when she recognized Race, looking so different, so worldly in the tailored suit. A little fever of excitement began licking through her veins, bringing a sheen of pleasure to her eyes. All thought of Mrs. Perez's importance as a wealthy client on the verge of spending a lot of money with Vanessa's firm flew right out of her head. Without even a glance at the woman, Vanessa stood up to greet Race, a hesitant smile of welcome spreading across her face.

"Hello, Race." Her voice was softly husky.

When he started across the room, Vanessa sensed something wasn't quite right. His dark gaze seemed fixed, and he walked with a kind of stiffness. The lazy smile that lifted the corners of his mouth seemed slightly dreamy.

"Happy anniversary, darlin'," he drawled, and raised the unopened magnum of champagne he was carrying. "I thought we'd celebrate the occasion."

Confusion clouded her expression. What was the matter with him? Vanessa thought. This

99

wasn't their anniversary. They'd been married in March—not July.

"Who is this?" Mrs. Perez inquired, inspecting Race with growing interest, not too old to appreciate his innately virile looks.

"Race Cantrell," Race introduced himself when Vanessa was slow on the uptake.

"How nice that he remembered your anniversary, Mrs. Cantrell," the woman stated with a trace of envy. "Unfortunately, I have to start dropping hints at least a month in advance if I expect Mr. Perez to remember ours."

"I've always been good with dates, haven't I, darlin'?" Race insisted with that same drawling intonation in his voice that was out of character.

When he curved an arm around her waist and hugged her to his side in an amorous display of affection, Vanessa was close enough to catch the potent smell of liquor on his breath. A raw frustration irritated her nerve ends as she realized Race was drunk. She had to get him away from Mrs. Perez before her client discovered his sodden condition.

"Would you excuse us for a minute, Mrs. Perez?" Vanessa murmured, conscious that more and more of his weight was leaning on her, warning her that he was none too steady on his feet.

Slipping an arm around his waist, she hoped it would look like a display of affection to Mrs. Perez rather than an attempt to support Race. As she directed him to her private office, she understood why he had walked so stiffly. It had been an instinctive attempt to keep himself from staggering drunkenly.

By the time she was able to steer him into her office, Vanessa was simmering with anger. He had come so close to embarrassing her in front of an important client. It was unforgivable for him to show up at her place of business half-stoned.

Angrily she pushed his hand off her waist and moved rigidly away from him to shut the door. Out of the corner of her eye she noticed that Race swayed for an instant without her support while his dazed glance looked around, trying to find her. She pressed her lips together in disgust.

"What's the idea of barging into my shop like this?" Vanessa accused; her voice trembled with the effort to keep it low so it wouldn't carry outside the private office. "Did you do it deliberately to try to hurt my business?"

"I don't know what you're talking about." His frown had a blankness to it, but there was a keen narrowing of his gaze.

"You're drunk—that's what I'm talking about," she snapped.

"I've been drinking," Race conceded with a little shrug of his wide shoulders. "After I started celebrating on my own, I decided to come get you." Again that lax smile curved his mouth.

Vanessa felt the pull of its warmth even though she knew it was liquor-induced. It rankled. "Why don't you go somewhere and sober up?" she bit out impatiently.

"I can't do that." He shook his head slowly, and lifted the champagne bottle again. "You and I have to celebrate our anniversary."

"You're so drunk that you don't even know what day this is, let alone what month!" Vanessa declared in disgust. "Today isn't our wedding anniversary, Race. That was in March."

He clicked his tongue at her in mock reproval. "Silly girl," he chided. "How could you have forgotten such an important event? Today is the anniversary of our divorce."

Her shocked glance ran to the wall calendar, the date leaping off the month's sheet. In the light of her recent doubt about the validity of her reasons for leaving him, it seemed impossible that she had forgotten.

"Come on." Race lurched slightly toward her and took her by the arm. "You and I are going to go out and celebrate the momentous occasion together—for old times' sake."

He spoke slowly and concisely to avoid slurring his words. He had himself so well under control that it was difficult for Vanessa to tell how much he'd had to drink. Hanging back, she resisted his attempt to drag her to the door.

"I can't go with you now," she protested. "I have a client outside, waiting for me. I can't just walk out and leave her."

"What's the difference?" Race challenged, swaying a little as he stopped to look at her. "You walked out and left me. I was your husband. She's just a customer. I'll get rid of her for you."

As he let go of her arm, Vanessa realized he

intended to carry out his statement. She darted forward to get between Race and the door and prevent him from getting to Mrs. Perez. In his condition, she wasn't sure what Race might tell the woman. She spread her hands across the front of his chest to stop him, and silently appealed to him to come to his senses.

"Race, please don't make a scene?" she asked.

"Are you coming with me now?" he countered. "I've made dinner reservations at Antoine's. I remember how long it takes you to get dressed up."

It was a subtle kind of blackmail, Vanessa realized. If she didn't agree to go with him, he was going to cause trouble with Mrs. Perez. The taunting gleam in his dark eyes informed Vanessa that he wasn't so inebriated that he didn't know he was coercing an agreement from her. She ground her teeth together, stifling her irritation.

"All right," Vanessa gave in grudgingly. "Wait here while I make some excuse to Mrs. Perez."

"I'm coming with you—to make sure you don't change your mind," Race asserted with a narrowed look that showed a lack of trust.

"It isn't necessary." But she saw the aggressively male thrust of his jaw and recognized that she couldn't talk him out of accompanying her. "Mrs. Perez is my client, so let me handle it," Vanessa insisted.

He made a mocking little bow of acquiescence and let her precede him out of the private office. As Vanessa approached the sofa, she was conscious that Race had paused by Carla's desk to sit unsteadily on the edge, the champagne bottle cradled in the crook of his arm. Mrs. Perez was standing and smoothing on a pair of silk gloves to hide the age spots on her hands.

"I'm sorry I kept you waiting." Vanessa started out with an apology, still searching for an adequate excuse.

"That's quite all right," the woman replied. "I hadn't realized how late it was. My daughter and her husband are coming for dinner, so perhaps we can continue this tomorrow—say, around two?"

It seemed incredible that after being so difficult to please all afternoon, Mrs. Perez was suddenly being so amenable. Vanessa couldn't believe her luck.

"Two o'clock will be fine." She nodded a slightly dazed agreement and automatically accompanied the woman to the shop door.

"Happy anniversary!" Mrs. Perez offered the salutation with a brief smile as she walked out the door.

When Vanessa turned back into the room, Race slid off the corner of the desk and clutched at it for support. Clearly Carla didn't know what to make of him or what his relationship was to Vanessa. She kept darting sideways glances at him.

"Thank you for the use of your desk." Race winked at the girl, aware that she was too flustered to reply. "Has anyone told you lately that you're an attractive girl?"

Carla actually turned red at his implied compliment and the sensually lazy smile that accompanied it. Then Race aimed himself at Vanessa and crossed the room, putting one foot in front of the other as if walking some invisible line. He paused barely long enough to slip a hand under her arm and propel her to the door Mrs. Perez had just exited through.

"We'll go to your apartment first so you can change," he stated. "Then we'll open this bottle of champagne and start celebrating."

Vanessa twisted in his grasp to look over her shoulder at her wide-eyed secretary. "Will you lock up for me, Carla?" she asked, and received a mute nod of affirmation.

Walking out of the air-conditioned shop into the oppressive heat and humidity of the Louisiana summer climate was like walking from a freezer into a steam room. Race reeled against her, affected by the moist blast of heat, and wrapped an arm around her shoulders to give him balance.

"Hold this." He thrust the champagne bottle at her. "I gotta find my keys."

Vanessa staggered as Race leaned more of his weight on her. "Where are you parked?" she asked.

A deep frown furrowed his brow as he tried to recall. "It can't be hard to find," Race assured her. "It was the only truck in the lot. I remember that."

"We'll take my car," she stated. "You're in no condition to be driving anyway."

With an arm around his waist to guide him, she directed him toward the stall where her car was parked. His coordination was deteriorating in the hot and humid air. He bumped his head twice as he tried to bend his tall frame into her low sports car. As soon as Vanessa had him safely installed in the passenger seat and the champagne bottle on his lap, she hurried around to the driver's side and slipped behind the wheel.

"Do you still have that blue dress?" Race turned his head to watch her as she started the car and reversed out of the parking stall. "The one with the silver belt?"

Vanessa knew precisely which dress he meant. It was a powder-blue chiffon, soft and flowing as whipped cream. It had been his favorite dress; now it was hidden in the back of her closet.

"No," she lied. It was slowly sinking in that if he wasn't drunk, he wouldn't have come to see her. It became a matter of pride. If he didn't want to be with her when he was sober, she didn't want to wear something to please him when he was drunk.

"That's too bad." He wore a sad frown of regret. "I wanted you to wear that tonight."

"For old times' sake," she murmured caustically, but Race didn't catch the bitter note of sarcasm.

Vanessa had no intention of going anywhere with him that evening, but this wasn't the time or place to argue with him. Race was already two sheets to the wind, and it was the first time she'd ever seen him when he'd had too much to drink.

It was a short drive from her shop to the apartment, although the traffic in the French Quarter added time to it. She helped Race out of the car, despite his attempt to shrug aside her offer of assistance. She was irritated and impatient with him for being in this intoxicated condition, but it accomplished nothing to let him see.

Once she had maneuvered him inside her apartment, she sat him down in one of the chairs and closed the door. Race started to get up when she moved toward the kitchen.

"You just stay there," Vanessa ordered. "I'm going to put on some coffee and see if I can't sober you up."

He subsided into the chair, his muscled body loose and unnaturally relaxed by his alcoholic consumption. Vanessa smothered a sigh of irritation and entered the kitchen. She added two extra scoops of coffee grounds to the pot to make it doubly strong. As she reached to take a cup from the shelf, a prickly sensation ran across the back of her neck, warning her that she was being watched. She turned to find Race in the doorway, still holding the magnum of champagne.

"You'd better start getting ready," he insisted.

"After the coffee's made." She pretended to go along with his plans. Race looked so compellingly attractive in the dark suit that she wished she was going out for the evening with him. There was a deep, tearing longing to be with him. Maybe after he had sobered up—if he still wanted to take her—she'd go out with him.

Pain flickered in his dark eyes as he studied her. "Why can't you love me the way I am, Vanessa?" Race questioned thickly, and her lips parted on a painful breath. "Why did you try to change me?"

"I didn't," Vanessa denied, but she realized his accusation was true.

"No." He shook his head slowly. "You wanted me to be different. You kept trying to turn me into a replica of my father."

"Not really," she protested weakly, because she had been guilty of that, in a sense. "It was just that . . . your company was going under and—"

"But it didn't go under," Race interrupted. "It was pretty rough going there for a while. I practically had to start from scratch, but . . ." He left that sentence unfinished, returning to his original subject. "You knew what I was like before you married me. I explained about my work. You said you understood."

Vanessa avoided his accusing eyes. "I know," she admitted. "I thought I could handle it, but the uncertainty . . ." Her voice trailed off, leaving her inability to cope with it unsaid.

"So you left me." The corners of his mouth were pulled down by a grim smile, which abruptly slanted. "And now, we have a divorce to celebrate."

His sudden change of mood, switching from solemn to lightheartedly indifferent to their breakup, forced Vanessa to remember it was pointless to attempt a serious conversation, when Race was unlikely to remember what was said. A raw frustration raged through her. It wasn't fair. This was the first time they had discussed their differences without shouting at each other and resorting to bitter insults. Why did it have to happen when he was drunk?

"Yes, and now we're divorced," she snapped at him in agitation, and stared at the coffeecup in her hand.

Behind her, the coffeemaker gurgled its last time. She turned to fill the cup, catching Race's movement into the kitchen out of the corner of her eyes. He stopped at the counter beside her and leaned a hip against it, seeking the support of something solid to hide his weaving unsteadiness.

"It's getting late," Race warned her. "If you're going to be ready in time to make our dinner reservations at Antoine's, you'd better get a move on."

"I know." Vanessa played along with him as she filled the cup with steaming black coffee from the pot. Turning, she took the champagne bottle from him and put the coffeecup in his hand. "Drink that."

Obediently he raised it to his mouth and brought it sharply down at the first scalding taste. "It's too hot." He set the cup on the counter, then let his gaze travel over her figure in a stripping study. "Want me to draw your bathwater?"

"No thanks. I'll do it myself," she refused, conscious of the uneven rush of blood through her veins at the knowing intimacy of his look. "You just drink your coffee and let me worry about getting ready in time."

"Nope." Race shook his head. "If I let you dawdle, we'll never make it there by seven. I learned that the hard way."

Once it had been true that she had taken an unconscionably long time getting ready to go out for an evening, but that had changed since Vanessa had started her own business and was forced to utilize her time more efficiently.

"That isn't true anymore," Vanessa replied. "If necessary, I can bathe and change in twenty minutes flat."

Race eyed her with a skeptical tilt of his head. "I don't want to take any chances, just the same. I'll help you undress."

Trapped by the cabinet and the wall, Vanessa wasn't able to elude his hands when they reached for the front of her lavender-mint blouse. She managed to push his fingers away from the buttons and found herself in the middle of a grappling contest.

"I don't need any help, Race," she protested with a trace of anger, but he was unfazed by it as he managed to pull one side of her blouse free from the waistband of her skirt. Her attempts to thwart his efforts were only succeeding in goading Race to continue, amused by her struggles. In a fit of exasperation, Vanessa sought a compromise. "Look," she reasoned, throwing up her hands in defeat. "If you promise to drink that coffee, I'll get undressed and take my bath right now. Is that a deal?"

Like a sulking child who has discovered it isn't fun to taunt his sibling anymore, Race brought his hands back to his sides. "I'll drink the coffee if that's what it's going to take for you to get ready for dinner," he agreed, and picked up the cup, waiting for her to move before he sipped at it.

Vanessa made an absent attempt to smooth her partially disarranged clothes as she walked past him toward the living room and ultimately to the bedroom with its private bath. She paused in the archway.

"I want you to drink more than just that one cup," she ordered curtly. "It's going to take the whole pot before you are even close to being sober."

Race inclined his head with exaggerated formality, mocking her while apparently bowing to her wishes. Vanessa didn't like the way he was grinning.

In the quiet of her bedroom, frissons of relief trembled through her. She hadn't realized how tense she had been in Race's company until she was alone. A hot, relaxing bath became infinitely appealing. Besides, as single-minded as Race was on the subject, he was likely to come into the room and dump her in the bathtub if she didn't voluntarily take one.

Before undressing, Vanessa went into the bathroom and stoppered the tub. When she had the tap water adjusted to a comfortably hot temperature, she left the water to run and returned to the bedroom. No sound was coming from the living room or kitchen. Vanessa wasn't sure whether that was a good sign or not. She hesitated a second longer before walking to the closet for her rose-pink flowered caftan.

By the time she had undressed and hung up her clothes, the tub was filled with water. She hooked the caftan on the brass peg behind the bathroom door and stepped gingerly into the tub, slowly submersing her body in the water.

As she was soaping the large natural sponge, Vanessa heard a sudden noise somewhere in the apartment. With a puzzled frown she held herself motionless to listen, unable to identify the single short sound. When nothing followed it, she decided that there was no need for alarm.

She began rubbing the sponge over her neck and shoulders, but her enjoyment of the sensuous feeling was broken by the sound of footsteps in her bedroom, approaching the bathroom door. Her widened gaze flew to the door. She hadn't locked it. There had never been any reason to in the past, since she'd always been alone in the apartment.

"Hey, Vanessa?" Race seemed to pound awkwardly on the door. "Open up, will ya?"

"What do you want?" She sat motionlessly, the sponge resting on the water's surface.

"Let me in." A second later, the doorknob rattled, not quite making a full turn to release the latch.

Vanessa stood up, mindless of the bathwater that sloshed over the side of the tub at the suddenness of her movement. She was reaching for the large towel on the brass rack when the door opened and Race lurched into the bathroom. In one hand he was carrying two wineglasses from her cupboard, and the other held the champagne bottle with frothy bubbles foaming from the neck opening to drip on the floor.

His gaze roamed the length of her naked body, taking in the firm roundness of her breasts with their rose-brown nipples and the slender curve of her hips. His look heated her flesh more than the bathwater had.

"You've filled out some," Race observed with a pleased look.

Damn him for saying that when he was drunk, Vanessa thought in annoyed anger. She finished her grab for the towel and stepped out of the tub to hold it lengthwise in front of her, hiding her nudity. Her action produced a low nasty laugh from Race.

"Such outdated modesty," he taunted. "We were married. There isn't an inch of your body that I don't know intimately."

"We aren't married now," Vanessa reminded him tersely. "I prefer to bathe in private, if you don't mind."

"Oh, but I do," Race countered. "I decided we might as well get our celebration started."

He tipped the champagne bottle to fill the two glasses held between his fingers by their stems, but his pouring aim was none too good. Most of the bubbling wine spilled onto the floor. The glasses were only half-full when he set the bottle on the washstand.

"A toast to the fourth anniversary of our divorce." He handed Vanessa one of the glasses and lifted the other in a salute.

It wasn't an occasion that she wanted to drink to, so she simply held her glass. Her fingers tightened around the cool glass stem, their pressure nearly snapping it, as Race tossed his wine down in one gulp and reached for the champagne bottle to fill it again. He took another swallow before he noticed she hadn't touched hers.

"What's the matter?" he demanded. "Why aren't you drinking to our divorce? It's what you wanted."

"I'm well aware of what I wanted," she snapped at his cutting reminder. "I don't need you to tell me." She shoved the wineglass onto the sink counter and stepped angrily toward him. "Right now, what I want is for you to get out of my bathroom."

Vanessa laid the flat of her hand in the middle of his chest and pushed him backward. Race didn't have the balance to resist. With a glass of champagne in one hand and the bottle in the other, he couldn't stop her from pushing him out of the bathroom and slamming the door in his face. This time, Vanessa locked it and stood trembling for a moment.

Bitter tears filled her eyes, blinding her so she couldn't see. She pressed a fist to her mouth to smother the sobs while she hugged the towel tightly around her ribs.

Chapter Seven

Vanessa had no idea how long she lay in the tub letting the bathwater soak away the hurt. The water was cool when she finally climbed out of it and toweled herself dry. She slipped the caftan over her head and took a deep, calming breath before she walked out of the bathroom, bracing herself for another meeting with Race.

The apartment seemed strangely quiet. She paused in the bedroom, tipping her head at a listening angle. A shiver of alarm prickled her skin as it suddenly occurred to her that Race might have left. The thought of him staggering drunkenly down some narrow street roused a concern for his safety that overrode the angry bitterness.

"Race?" Vanessa called his name as she hurried into the living room.

There was no answer, but her running steps were halted when she saw him sprawled across the sofa and coffee table. An empty wineglass dangled loosely from his fingers, hanging upside down. The champagne bottle had fallen and was lodged between two cushions. Some of the sparkling wine had been spilled, absorbed by the carpet. Seething with a mixture of frustration and angry concern, Vanessa realized that Race had drunk most of the bottle before he had passed out.

Crossing to the sofa, she took the glass from his hand and rescued the champagne bottle from the cushions. His dark head was drooping to one side at an awkward angle. After she set the bottle and glass on an end table, Vanessa studied him for an irritated moment, her foot unconsciously tapping the carpeted floor. For a spiteful moment she was tempted to leave him like that, knowing full well that he'd wind up with a stiff neck and a sore back.

As she studied his strong male features, an overwhelming tenderness surged through her. There was nothing about him that remotely resembled a little boy, yet there was a need to comfort and take care of him.

It wasn't too difficult to swing his legs off the coffee table where they had been propped, but it was like trying to lift a one-hundred-and-eighty-pound deadweight when Vanessa attempted to maneuver him into a horizontal position on the couch. After a couple of unsuccessful tries that left her breathing hard, she accomplished her mission.

Race was too long for the sofa, his feet extending over the end, but Vanessa knew she didn't have a hope of getting him into the bedroom. Plumping a yarn-fringed throw pillow, she tucked it under his head. She took off his shoes, removed his tie, and unbuttoned the top three buttons of his shirt. Race groaned once but never stirred.

Taking a spare blanket from the closet, Vanessa spread it over him, then sat for a minute on a narrow edge of the sofa cushion. Her fingers lightly smoothed the rumpled mass of dark hair that fell onto his forehead.

It seemed strange to discover that tonight was the first time Vanessa felt Race had needed her. He had always seemed so irritatingly self-sufficient, so damned proud and self-confident. Not once had he ever leaned on her, not even when his company had been on the verge of bankruptcy and they'd lost all personal property of any value.

When she walked out on him and filed for divorce, Race had bitterly accused her of leaving him when he needed her the most. But Vanessa had never believed that he really meant it. A stillness came over her now as she suddenly realized the possible significance of that. Had she left Race because he hadn't shown that he needed her? And if he didn't need her, didn't it equate that he didn't love her either? Or was it just another reason to add to the string she'd already listed?

With a confused sigh, she straightened from the sofa. What was the use of conducting a postmortem? It wouldn't change anything. After four years, it was foolish to think there was any chance they might get back together. Maybe Race had the right idea after all. Maybe she should drink until she passed out, too.

Vanessa went into the kitchen and opened the refrigerator door, but she didn't touch the bottle of wine. She took out the leftover chicken casserole from the night before and put it in the oven to warm.

After eating a light meal and washing up the dishes, she curled up in the armchair in the living room and turned on the reading lamp, making sure the light was turned away from Race. She picked up a book and opened to the chapter she'd been reading, but she spent more time watching Race than she did reading. He was dead to the world. It seemed unlikely he would waken until morning.

By ten o'clock, Vanessa was yawning. Setting the book aside, she switched off the lamp and made her way to the bedroom in the dark. A few minutes later, she had changed into her short nightie and was sliding under the covers. She fell asleep almost instantly.

In the middle of the night, Vanessa was awakened by a loud crash followed by the muffled curses of a man. The first thing that flashed through her mind was that a burglar was in her apartment. She reached for the telephone on the bedstand to call the police. Shocked into full alertness by fear, Vanessa suddenly recognized Race's voice, and her hand came away from the stand before it had reached its objective.

The matching robe to her nightie was lying on the antique sea trunk at the foot of the four-poster bed. Swinging out of bed, Vanessa snatched it up as she hurried toward the living room. When she reached the door, a lamp was switched on, and she saw Race setting it upright after obviously knocking it over.

"Are you all right?" she asked anxiously.

His hand was in front of his face, shielding his eyes from the glare of the light. "Just dandy," he growled. "Would you tell me where the hell the bathroom is in this place?"

Vanessa guessed that he felt like death warmed over, and had to hide a smile. "It's this way," she murmured, certain he wouldn't appreciate her humor at this moment.

Holding his head as if it weighed a ton, Race walked gingerly in her direction. She had a glimpse of his haggard and drawn features as he passed her, heading straight for the bathroom door. He looked terrible—and probably felt worse, she guessed.

"Is there anything I can do—?" The bathroom door was shut before she could complete her offer of assistance.

There was a slight drooping of her shoulders as she stared at the closed door. Race wasn't drunk now. He didn't need her help. Her lips thinned tightly together in a straight line. With more than a trace of anger, she took off her robe and tossed it on the trunk before climbing back into bed and turning her back to the bathroom door.

Several minutes went by before Race came out. She could hear him moving about in the bedroom, but she wasn't about to ask if she could help him find whatever it was he was looking for. She lay rigidly in bed, hating him in that crazy way her emotion toward him kept flip-flopping.

Almost simultaneously, the bedcovers were pulled off her shoulder as the mattress sank under the sudden addition of Race's weight. Vanessa started to roll onto her back, only to feel his hand push at her.

"Move over," Race commanded with open irritation.

Vanessa didn't have much choice as his muscular body forcibly pushed her to the far side of the bed. "What do you think you're doing?" she demanded, propping herself up on her elbows to glare at him in the semidarkness.

He was already settling into a comfortable position. "If that sofa was the best you could do, you should have at least covered my feet." He grumbled the complaint with ill-humor. "They're freezing."

"I did cover your feet," Vanessa retorted. "It isn't my fault if you kicked the blanket off."

"Shut up and go to sleep." Race burrowed his face into the pillow, letting it muffle some of the harshness in his voice. "If you're too damned prudish to share the bed with me, then you go sleep on the sofa."

"Maybe I'll do that," she flared indignantly.

"Maybe you'd better," he snarled. "I just might rape you in the middle of the night."

His tone of voice derided the possibility, stinging her with its undisguised contempt. She let her elbows slide out from under her to lie on her back and stare at the ceiling. A stubbornness set in that would not let her abandon her own bed for the dubious comfort of the sofa. But she found it nearly impossible to go back to sleep.

Race didn't have the same difficulty. Within minutes she could tell by his even, shallow breathing that he was asleep. When he shifted in the bed, Vanessa felt the familiar abrasion of his bare, hair-roughened legs against hers. She had suspected he was wearing only his Jockey shorts, as had been his habit when they were married. The contact with his hard flesh confirmed it.

Gradually the familiarity of having him in bed returned and her body began to relax. Then Vanessa was drifting off to sleep.

The alarm shrilled its wake-up call through the room, shattering Vanessa's peaceful sleep. Race had his arm flung across her waist, weighting her down. He stirred when she pushed it off to roll to the edge of the bed and reach for the alarm clock.

"For Crissake, shut that damned thing off," Race said in a half-muttered moan of protest.

Vanessa pushed in the little knob to silence it, then lay on her stomach, propped up with her elbows while she tried to orient herself to the early-morning light spilling through the window. She blinked her eyes several times to free them of their sticky sleepiness. A huge yawn claimed her as she lifted the covers to climb out of bed.

"Do you have to bounce on the bed like that?" Race complained, his voice muffled.

With a confused frown, Vanessa turned to look at him. She had *dragged* herself out of bed. How could he accuse her of *bouncing*? His face was half-buried under the pillow, and the covers were halfway up his back. All she could see of him was the back of his head where his dark, nearly black hair grew shaggily down his neck, and the sinewed contours of his sun-bronzed shoulders with his ridged spine running down the center.

It took her a second to realize he was undoubtedly hung-over after all the alcohol he'd consumed last night. All sound and motion became magnified to him. Vanessa reacted with a callous disregard for his problem, deciding it served him right.

She disappeared into the bathroom, coming out a few minutes later with her face washed and her teeth brushed. Race appeared to be once more sleeping soundly as she walked to the closet to select what she was going to wear that day. After sifting through the hanging clothes, she finally decided on the straightforward simplicity of a sunny yellow dress with capped sleeves and buttoned front, trimmed with white piping.

As an accessory, Vanessa took a white neck scarf with yellow polka dots from a dresser drawer. Clean underclothes were in another drawer. She removed a set, and a half-slip, then pushed the drawer closed with her hip.

"Do you have to make so much noise?" Race growled from the bed.

"I'm not." Vanessa finally responded to his unwarranted grumbling.

"You don't have to shout, either," he muttered, not moving from his position in the bed, as though any motion was to be avoided at all costs. "Would you pull the window blind?"

"Is the light hurting your eyes?" she asked sweetly, but walked to the window to pull the shade.

"What the hell do you think?" Race replied more forcefully than his other complaints had been issued. There was an immediate groan of regret at the disturbance it caused within.

A smile played with her lips. Vanessa felt a malicious glee at his discomfort after the way he'd treated her last night with such scornful disinterest. She wanted him to feel as rotten and abused as she had last night.

After she had dressed and put on her makeup, she went into the kitchen and fixed a full pot of coffee instead of her usual half. She breakfasted on orange juice, toast, and coffee. When she had finished her third cup, it was time to leave for the shop.

Before leaving the apartment, Vanessa stopped in the bedroom doorway. Race was still sleeping, his position unchanged. She hesitated, almost turning away, then changed her mind.

"Race." Her voice was very matter-of-fact. "I'm leaving now." There was no movement, no indication he heard her, but Vanessa continued just the same. "The coffee is hot and there's tomato juice and orange juice in the refrigerator."

Her only reply was a grunted acknowledgment. With a flicker of irritation, Vanessa studied his sleeping male form a second longer, wondering why she didn't roll him out of bed and show him the door instead of letting him stay in her apartment while she was gone. Of course, she didn't do it, and locked the apartment door behind her as she left.

The first two hours in the morning, Vanessa always spent catching up on the paperwork and making out the billings for Carla to type. She was checking a supplier's invoice and verifying she'd been given the proper discount when she was interrupted by a knock on the door. "Come in." For a split second she thought it might be Race, coming by to apologize for his inebriated condition yesterday—and perhaps even thank her for the hospitality she hadn't been obligated to extend to him.

But the door was opened by her assistant decorator, Peter Benoit. A charming smile was pinned on his handsome Gallic features. With his typical flair for the dramatic, he was dressed in jet-black slacks that hugged his slim length and a coral silk shirt with a matching black-and-coral ascot around his neck. He gave the appearance of a dandy, but Vanessa had seen him slopping wallpaper paste side by side with fabric hangers with total disregard for his created image of never dirtying his hands with "work."

"Do you have a few minutes, Vanessa?" Despite the polite question, he was walking right into her office, taking it for granted that she had the time to spare to speak to him.

"Have a seat." She hid a smile and motioned to the velvet chair in front of her desk.

"I tried to catch you last night, but Carla said you left early yesterday." He lowered himself gracefully into the chair and crossed a leg over his knee. "I wasn't sure you'd be in this morning."

"Why not?" Vanessa arched a delicate brow in mild surprise.

"Carla mentioned that you'd left with a man." He didn't try to hide the curious speculation in his expression. "I understand there was talk of an anniversary. Have you been keeping something from us?"

Carla wouldn't have dreamed of prying into Vanessa's private life, no matter how eaten up with curiosity she was, but Peter had no such compunction.

"The man you're referring to happened to be my ex." Vanessa didn't see any point in dodging the question. "And yesterday was the anniversary of our divorce."

"So you went out to celebrate," Peter concluded. "Tell me, were the old flames still burning?"

"No, I didn't celebrate, and no, I didn't discover any old fires still burning last night," she could answer truthfully as she folded her hands together and rested them on her desktop. "Is this what you came in to talk to me about?"

He chuckled softly. "You have a very tactful way of pushing people's noses out of your personal life. Mine has been properly snubbed," he assured her, unoffended. "I found out yesterday that a love seat I ordered for Mrs. Steinhope is no longer being manufactured. I've managed to track down another that's almost identical, but it's very cheaply made. I know substituting inferior-quality items goes against your policy, but Mrs. Steinhope has her heart set on this particular piece. I've explained to her that it will probably fall apart in a couple of years, but she insists she wants it anyway. I wanted to clear it with you first."

Vanessa firmly shook her head to veto the idea. "When it falls apart in two years, I can guarantee that Mrs. Steinhope will forget she said any such thing." She flipped through her Rolodex and jotted down a man's name and phone number, giving it to Peter. "This man rebuilds and restores period furniture. He does excellent work. Perhaps you could contract with him to build a love seat in the style and specifications that she wants."

"You're always able to cope with a situation,

regardless of what it is," Peter marveled wryly. "You take everything in stride."

There was nothing to be gained by contradicting him, but Vanessa knew he was wrong. She hadn't known how to cope with married life, and it had ended up in shambles. But his remark seemed to point again to the possibility that money problems and the absence of security had not been the main causes for her divorce. Perhaps she had been closer to the truth last night when she discovered Race had never really needed her before.

With Peter's departure, Vanessa turned back to her paperwork. The day settled into its usual routine. Yet, all day long there was a persistent expectancy that Race would stop by or at least call. His truck was parked somewhere in the vicinity, so he wouldn't have to go out of his way to see her.

After another long session with Mrs. Perez, Vanessa stayed later than usual to catch up with the backlog of work that had accumulated. It was after seven o'clock when she arrived at her apartment.

With leaden steps that matched her mood, she unlocked the door and crossed the threshold to enter the living room. She leaned against the closed door and slipped off her white summer heels.

"Do you always work this late?" Race spoke from the kitchen archway, startling Vanessa, her blood suddenly shooting through her veins.

She tried to cool the hot rush of pleasure as her gaze swept warmly over him. He was leaning casually against the archway, wearing the dark suit pants and the white shirt, without the jacket and tie, and looked for all the world like he belonged in the apartment.

"I thought you'd be gone." Vanessa voiced her first thought, forgetting that he'd asked a question.

"Do you want me to leave?" A dark brow was lifted in faint challenge.

The hint of antagonism in the air irritated Vanessa. She hadn't been expressing a wish, only voicing her thoughts, but Race had twisted the other meaning into it.

"I didn't say that," she retorted, and moved away from the door with her shoes dangling from her fingers by the heel straps.

"Do you want me to stay?" Race turned the question around.

That question was just as difficult to field as the first, because it meant expressing a desire for his company. Vanessa wasn't sure she wanted to expose herself to potential hurt. Avoiding his steady gaze, she walked to the sofa and dropped her shoes and purse on its cushions.

"Go or stay." She faked a shrug of indifference. "I'm sure you'll do as you like anyway. " She nervously smoothed a hand over her hair, checking to make sure it was still neatly in place. "How's your hangover?" A sixth sense informed her the instant Race pushed away from the arch to come into the living room.

"A few dull throbs here and there. Outside of that, I've recovered," he murmured, and stopped near the end of the sofa. "I'm surprised you didn't throw me out last night. You could have," he reminded her. "I wasn't in any condition to put up much of a struggle."

"Letting you sleep it off seemed the humane thing to do," Vanessa answered, because it seemed best not to let him know how much she had enjoyed looking after him—being needed by him. No doubt he would have scoffed and insisted he could have managed very well without her help.

"Have you eaten?" Race changed the subject.

"No," she admitted.

"Neither have I. We never did get to Antoine's for dinner last night. Shall I check to see if we can get reservations tonight? " he asked.

Vanessa thought he was making a joke until she looked at him and noticed his solemn expression. Last night, she had believed his choice of one of the most expensive and renowned restaurants in town had been prompted by a display of bravado. Last night, he'd been drunk. Right now, he looked sober.

"Have you been drinking again?" she accused. "You know you can't afford to go there."

"Can't I?" Race countered smoothly, then added as a bland afterthought, "No, I haven't been drinking."

Vanessa let the latter slide by, frowning at his curious response to her remark. "How could you afford it—unless . . ." She paused, her eyes widening on a sudden thought. "Did your well test out as a producer?"

There was a slight narrowing of his gaze as he considered her for a long second before answering. Then he deliberately avoided her eyes. "No, my well didn't test out."—His reply sounded almost guarded.

"I . . ." Vanessa started to tell him how sorry she was, but she could just imagine his reaction to any offer of sympathy from her. So she wiped away the disappointment she'd felt for him and tried to be offhand about the news. "That's too bad. But, like you said to Phillip, there's always another well to be drilled, and the next one, near Baton Rouge, might be a money-maker."

"Would you like it if I hit it big?" Race murmured, appearing to measure her reaction with his glance.

"What kind of a question is that?" Vanessa hid her puzzled frown behind a confused laugh. "Of course I'd be happy for you."

"Of course." His mouth twitched in a humorless line as he repeated her phrase with a trace of cynicism.

Vanessa bristled at his tone. "We may not have separated on the best of terms, but I still wish you every success in the world. I am not the selfish bitch that you make me out to be."

There was an amused lift of one eyebrow. "You never used to swear without blushing."

His remark didn't improve her temper. "You surely didn't expect that I would remain innocent and naive forever?" she retorted.

"I guess not," Race said with a kind of invisible shrug. "Since Antoine's is out, how does an oyster poor boy sound? I think my finances could stretch to that."

Vanessa blinked at the quantum leaps he was making: one minute practically insulting her, and the next, inviting her out to eat. It wasn't easy keeping up with his lightning changes of attitude and subject.

"It sounds good," she managed finally.

"Are your feet up to walking?" He glanced down at her bare toes curling into the carpeting in little-girl fashion. "Or should we drive?"

"We're just going right here in the French Quarter, aren't we?" At his affirmative nod, Vanessa reasoned, "It would take longer to find a place to park than it would to walk there. Even then, we'd probably end up walking a ways, so we might as well start out on foot."

"If you're game, so am I," Race agreed.

"Just give me a minute to get my shoes on." She retrieved them from the sofa cushion and leaned against the armrest to balance herself while she put them on.

Her feet were always a little swollen by the end of the day, so the sandaled heels didn't go on as easily as they had slipped off. Vanessa struggled to inch the strap over her heel, and nearly snapped a nail.

"You'd better let me do it," Race stated, and crouched down at her feet to take over the task.

Vanessa straightened, conscious of the nervous flutter in her stomach. His hand cupped the back of her ankle to support her foot while he pushed the shoe more firmly onto it. She couldn't help staring at the dark head bent over her foot, the thickness of his hair almost inviting the touch of her fingers. She curled them into the armrest, a disturbing heat spreading over her skin.

Race looked up as he tried to work the strap over her heel. A wickedly mocking light danced in his eyes as he met Vanessa's uneasy glance.

"Are you sure you aren't one of Cinderella's ugly stepsisters, and this slipper really doesn't belong to you?" he joked.

"It's mine," she said, and felt silly for responding seriously to a question he had issued in jest.

"That's what *she* said," Race mocked. A second later the strap slipped into position around her heel. "One down and one to go." He picked up the other shoe.

The heady fragrance of male after-shave lotion rose to stimulate her senses. Idly Vanessa let her gaze wander over the clean, strong line of his jaw before the significance of his smooth cheeks registered.

"You've shaved," she declared on a startled note.

"Yes." He sent her a mild glance.

"But how?" Even if he had used her razor, she certainly didn't have any men's after-shave lotion in her medicine cabinet.

"The usual way." The corners of his mouth deepened—he knew full well that wasn't what she meant. "No, I didn't dull your razor with my beard." Evidently discovering a trick to it, Race slipped the second shoe on her foot without much difficulty. "I used my own," he said, straightening to tower above her and looking down at her with a lazily intent study. "My shaving kit and a few other things were in my truck," he explained.

"Oh." Vanessa slid off the armrest to move a couple of steps away from him. "Did you have any trouble finding where you'd left your truck parked? You were a little uncertain about it yesterday."

"I didn't have any trouble, but then, I wasn't drunk today, either," he replied. "I started to stop in and see you, but I remembered you had an appointment this afternoon, so I decided against it."

"I wondered if you might," Vanessa admitted.

"Now that you've got your shoes on, shall we go eat?" He raised a hand, palm upward, in a gesture that invited Vanessa to take the lead.

An uneasy truce seemed to exist between them, but Vanessa was conscious of the strong undercurrents in the air around them and wondered how long it would last.

Chapter Eight

It was a sultry evening, a lowering sun laying a golden glow over the French Quarter of New Orleans. A lazy stroll was the accepted pace in the lingering summer-afternoon heat. Leaving the four-story apartment building with its block-long balcony decorated with ornate cast iron, they crossed the street to Jackson Square.

They wandered leisurely past the varied display of artworks, ranging from Quarter scenes to portraits, and paused for a couple of minutes to watch a caricaturist at work. The light touch of Race's hand on her waist directed Vanessa across the street again into the cool shadows of Pirate's Alley, so named because pirates were taken down this narrow corridor to the Cabildo Jail.

There didn't seem to be any need to talk as they wandered down the narrow passageway with St. Louis Cathedral rising on one side and the Cabildo on the other, once the meeting place of the Spanish legislature, now a historical museum. Vanessa had always felt a special attachment to the French Quarter. It was an area like no other, rich in history and steeped in romantic ambience.

The alley opened onto Royal Street. The guiding touch of Race's hand turned her onto it. This occasional contact, never constant or lasting for long, kept her awareness of him at high level. The strong, carved lines of his profile were always in her side vision, the tapered strength of his body always within inches of her. While her eyes enjoyed the Creole architecture of the Quarter, a unique blend of French and Spanish, the rest of the senses were attuned to Race.

Street musicians were giving an impromptu jazz performance on an adjacent corner, filling the air with the wailing upbeat music that had become synonymous with New Orleans. The quaint, picturesque buildings lining the straight, narrow streets were adorned with wrought-iron or cast-iron railings that relieved the otherwise severe architecture. Occasionally Vanessa caught a glimpse of a flagstoned courtyard beyond a building gate, an oasis of subtropical shrubbery and flowering plants amid all the brick and concrete.

They approached one of the many cafés in the Quarter that had both inside seating and sidewalk tables.

Race glanced at her, lifting a querying brow. "I thought we'd eat here. Do you want to sit outside or would you rather go in?" he asked.

"Let's sit outside," Vanessa said. "I like to watch the people."

With a nod of acceptance at her choice, Race guided her to an empty table. They were barely seated before the waiter appeared to offer them menus.

"I think we know what we want." Race refused the menu card and glanced at Vanessa to be certain they were in agreement about the meal. She nodded. "We'll both have your oyster poor boy."

"And to drink, sir?"

"I'll have a beer," Race ordered, and looked at her. "What would you like, Vanessa?"

"Iced tea, please."

With the departure of the waiter, there was an uneasy silence that Vanessa didn't know how to fill. She laced her fingers together atop the table and studied them, searching for something safe to say.

"How—?"

"Have—?"

They both spoke at the same time, and stopped to let the other finish. It seemed to break the tension. A low chuckle came from Race, while her lips relaxed into a slightly self-conscious smile.

"You first," Race said.

"I was just going to ask if you'd seen Phillip lately," she explained.

"I haven't seen him for a couple of weeks, but

137

I talked to him on the telephone yesterday —before I started celebrating," Race added, mockingly assuring her that he hadn't been drinking at the time. "He mentioned the two of you had dinner together last week sometime."

"Yes." Vanessa lowered her gaze, remembering the discussion she'd had with his father concerning their divorce and the uncertainties hindsight had given her. "He seemed like his old self."

"When I talked to him, he indicated he was concerned about you," Race informed her.

"About me?" she repeated nervously, and tried to appear as if she couldn't imagine what he was talking about.

"He was under the impression that you had some misgivings about your reasons for leaving me four years ago." He wouldn't release her from the keenness of his gaze.

Vanessa pressed her lips tightly together, feeling that his father had betrayed a confidence. "I didn't realize Phillip was going to carry tales."

"Do you have regrets?" Race pushed for an answer.

"Some," was all she was willing to admit. "I'm not sure anymore that I tried hard enough to make our marriage work. But when you're young, you have the tendency to put the emphasis on the wrong things."

"Such as?" he prompted.

Vanessa hesitated before answering, trying to gauge his mood, but Race appeared to be acutely interested in her response, rather than ready to treat it with his customary derisive mockery.

"Such as . . . losing our house. I don't think you ever understood the need I had for security." Because he was actually listening to her, Vanessa tempered her words with calm reason, not attacking him as she was guilty of doing at times. "I lost my parents at a critical age. One minute I was surrounded by everything that was dear and familiar to me . . . and in the next, it was gone. I was uprooted—without a home or family. I was forced to live with an older cousin, but I never felt that I belonged there. More than anything else, I wanted a home of my own, a place where I belonged—something solid where I could put down roots. It was a blow when I realized it obviously didn't mean anything to you, or you wouldn't have gambled it away."

"It was just a house," Race countered.

—"But it was more than walls and a roof to me," Vanessa insisted. "It was our home. I didn't think there could ever be another. Now my apartment is home. Maybe we could have found another place. I know you tried to convince me of that at the time."

"We could have."

"Probably," she conceded. "I guess I just didn't want to risk losing that one, too." She unlaced her fingers to rub them together. "Being in business for myself has taught me there are certain risks you have to take if you want to get ahead. But you don't have to risk everything."

"That's where you and I differ," he stated. "If you really believe in something, you should be willing to risk it all. And as for walls and a roof, they don't make a home. Love is the ingredient that makes a place into a home. Anywhere we lived would have been home to me."

But love had been a missing ingredient. He had not needed her or loved her. Vanessa would have pointed that out to him, but the waiter came with their sandwiches. After they were served, the opportunity was gone, and she was reluctant to bring up the subject again. Conversation waned while they consumed their sandwiches of succulent fried oysters mounded between halves of New Orleans-style French bread.

After they'd eaten the last crumb, they lingered over their cold drinks, too full to talk. Twilight was settling over the Vieux Carré and the old-fashioned streetlamps were flickering on when Race pushed his chair away from the table, taking the initiative to leave.

"Shall we start back?" he suggested.

"Sure." Vanessa scooted her chair back and stood up.

They wound their way through the tables to the outer edge of the sidewalk. The clop-clop of calked hooves sounded in the street behind them as a horse and carriage, empty of passengers, came alongside. Race pursed his lower lip, whistling shrilly and signaling the driver to stop.

"We'll ride back," he announced to Vanessa, and helped her into the carriage seat, telling the driver, "Jackson Square."

"The long way or the short way?" The driver drawled the question

"The long way." Race settled back in the seat

and casually draped an arm around her shoulders.

The carriage lurched forward as the harnessed horse pulled against the traces. His hand tightened its hold just below her shoulder bone to steady her until the carriage was rolling smoothly, then it relaxed a little while retaining firm possession. There was a sense of almost forbidden pleasure at sitting so close to him, able to feel the length of his thigh pressed against her leg and the warmth of his body flowing through to her and heating her flesh. Her pulse beat with an edge of excitement, stirred by his nearness.

The air was perfumed by the flowers bedecking the carriage and heightening the romance of the ride. Affected by the pervading mood, Vanessa stole a glance at Race. As if sensing her look, he turned his head, his gaze flicking to her lips for a disturbing second before traveling upward to meet her look. There was a slow movement of his mouth into a faint smile that seemed to warm her all the way to her toes. There was a very loverlike quality to the moment.

The long way to Jackson Square was all too short. After helping her out of the carriage, Race paid the driver and followed her into the apartment building. Vanessa wanted to ask him in, but she was hesitant, not wanting a beautiful evening spoiled by bitter words. And the unspoken truce they'd been observing seemed too good to last.

Her indecision was ended when Race took it

for granted she was inviting him in. "Shall we have coffee on the balcony?" he suggested while she was unlocking the apartment door.

"That's a good idea," Vanessa agreed.

While she was in the kitchen making the coffee, she felt the same nervous excitement that she'd known when they were first dating—that wondrous uncertainty and anticipation of what was to come. It was difficult to tell her heart to be still, that it wasn't that way between them anymore.

As she was setting two cups on a round serving tray, the telephone rang in the living room. She moved to answer it, but just as she reached the archway, it was cut off in mid-ring. Race had picked up the receiver, answering it in an impersonal voice that quickly changed when he recognized the calling party.

"Hello, Dad," he said, and glanced sideways to see her poised in the archway. Vanessa couldn't help wondering what Phillip was thinking because Race had answered the phone. "Vanessa is fixing coffee," Race said in an apparent explanation for being the one who answered. The next time he spoke, his voice sounded more guarded. "No, I haven't. I'm not going to—at least, not yet." Without the benefit of hearing Phillip's question, his response made no sense to her. "I will. Do you want to talk to Vanessa?" His query was followed by a slight pause. "I'll tell her. Good-bye."

"That was evidently your father," she guessed the obvious.

"He was just calling to say hello," Race said

without elaborating on his brief conversation with him. "Is the coffee ready yet?"

"It should be." Vanessa glanced over her shoulder and noticed the brewing light was off on the coffeemaker.

"Need any help?"

"No, I can manage." She half-turned to reenter the kitchen. "You go ahead. I'll be right out."

After filling the cups with freshly brewed coffee, Vanessa carried the tray through the living room to the balcony doors. Race stepped forward to open them for her. In addition to the two wrought-iron chairs with removable cushions on her portion of the apartment balcony, there was a white wrought-iron table Vanessa set the tray on. Race dodged a hanging basket to take a cup from the tray, and walked to the railing to drink it. She carried hers over as well and leaned a shoulder against an intricately scrolled upright support.

"You have quite a view." Race stood with his legs slightly spread apart, facing the rail.

Vanessa let her gaze make a slow arc of the scene before them. The main spire of St. Louis Cathedral was thrust toward the purpling blue of an evening sky, flanked by smaller twin spires. In the center of the square across the street, the statue of General Andrew Jackson sat atop a rearing horse, his hat lifted in a perpetual salute to the city he helped save. From the balcony, there was a glimpse of the Café du Monde and the French Market, while city lights were reflected on the waters of the Mississippi River just beyond the levee.

"Yes, it is impressive," Vanessa agreed.

Below them, the city's nightlife was wakening, yet they remained curiously removed from it, untouched by the noise and the activity. It was somnolent and quiet on the balcony; isolated. Vanessa was very conscious of being alone with Race. She sipped at her coffee, feeling the quivering awareness.

Race thoughtfully trailed a hand across the railing. "How does that quote go? 'What light from yonder window breaks?'" He glanced at her, showing uncertainty in his expression that he had it right.

Recognition flashed instantly. "'Wherefore art thou, Romeo?'" she quoted absently, tossing off the famous line from Shakespeare's *Romeo and Juliet* without any dramatic inflection.

"The famous balcony scene," Race concluded.

Their eyes met across the distance, and the air suddenly became charged with a thousand little electrical impulses, primitive and elemental. She had trouble breathing, her pulse skittering all over the place.

His mouth twisted with unexpected wryness. "Do you know what this reminds me of?"

"What?" There was a breathy catch to her voice. It didn't come out calm and unaffected the way she wanted it to sound.

"Standing here, looking at you, reminds me of the time when we were first dating," Race said, expressing virtually the same feeling she'd had earlier in the kitchen. "In the beginning, I was always wondering whether it was too early to put a move on you."

"And I was always wondering how far I was going to let you go," Vanessa admitted with a brief, husky laugh.

Instead of making a comment, Race extended his hand. "Are you through with your coffee?" He was offering to take her cup.

She had barely drunk any of it, but on an evening that was so warm, she lost her taste for drinking something hot. "Yes." She handed him the cup and turned her back to the rail, leaning back on it with her hands to watch him carry the two cups to the tray.

When he turned to walk back to the railing, a slow tightness began to climb inside her, moving up her throat. There was something about the way he was looking at her that made her blood run hot. He stopped in front of her, reaching with his fingertips to trace the curve of her cheekbone down to the delicate line of her jaw.

"Surely we're past that stage," he murmured huskily. "If I make a move now, how far will you let me go?"

His bluntness always managed to throw her off keel. This time was no exception. "I'm not sure," she managed, unable to be as candid as he was.

He let his hand slide to her shoulder while he reached with the other to take her left hand, effectively drawing her away from the balcony and closer to him. Her legs felt unsteady as he carried her fingers to the hard male line of his lips.

"Why don't you wear your wedding rings?" he asked, not taking his watchful eyes from her face while his lips formed the words against her curved fingers.

"I didn't think it was proper to wear them after we were divorced," Vanessa explained in a disturbed whisper.

"Other divorced women wear theirs," Race pointed out, still rubbing his mouth over the back of her fingers.

"I know, but I didn't feel I should. I didn't get rid of them," she added, in case he thought she might have sold them or given them away. "I keep them in my jewelry box."

"That's where they were." He lightly stressed the past tense.

Her eyes widened, amethyst-bright with confusion. "What do you mean?"

"I mean they aren't there now," he replied, which didn't really clear up anything.

"Then where . . . ?" Vanessa halted in midquestion as his hand left her shoulder and reached into the side pocket of his slacks. He had the interlocking set of wedding rings in his hand when he brought it out, the diamond solitaire engagement ring fitting inside a wide gold wedding band.

"I never asked you to take them off your finger," Race said as he slipped them back on and raised her hand to kiss the rings, as if resealing the vows that had been exchanged when they were placed on her finger by him. "I want you to wear them."

It had been years since she'd worn them—a little over four years, to be exact. They should have felt heavy or awkward on her finger; instead, they felt natural. She gave him a slightly dazed look.

"Any objection?" he asked at her continued silence.

"None," Vanessa murmured with a vague shake of her head.

"Last night I slept in your bed." His gaze moved possessively over her face, darting to each feature. "Tonight I want to sleep with you. Any objections?"

"Why?" She had to know his reason.

"Because it's driving me crazy to stand here, wanting to touch you and waiting for you to show me it's what you want, too," Race answered with an urgent edge to his voice. He watched her lips. "Do you?"

It seemed impossible to be seduced without being touched, but he was making love to her mentally, and her desire was aroused by it. Her need built into a physical ache that wouldn't go away.

"Yes," she admitted with a throb to her voice.

The disturbing darkness of his eyes was lightened by a spark of humor. "But not here on the balcony. Even for me, it's the wrong place." He curved her arm behind his back, then hugged her waist to mold her to his side. "Shall we adjourn to a place that offers more privacy? Say, the bedroom."

His remark seemed to take the heaviness from the moment, and leave in its place a naturalness. Vanessa was able to walk with him into the apartment without any awkward sensation of the deliberateness of the act.

When they entered the bedroom, she noticed the bed was made, evidently by Race after he had gotten up this morning. It was not as neatly done as she would have made it, but she was moved by the gesture. Race left her to walk over to the bed and turn down the covers. He sat down on the edge to take off his shoes, just as he had always done when they were married.

There was suddenly a comfortable pattern to everything that put her at ease, even though her pulse continued to race with anticipation. Vanessa untied the polka-dot neck scarf and tossed it absently onto the dresser top. Her shoes came off next as she walked to the closet, where she unbuttoned her dress and replaced it on its hanger. Wearing only a bra and a half-slip, she moved back to the mirror above the dresser and started to remove the pins securing her silky brown hair in its smooth coil.

His reflection appeared in the mirror behind hers. "Let me do that." Race volunteered his services for the task.

Vanessa brought her hands down and watched him begin deftly removing the pins. Gradually her eyes drifted closed while she savored the sensation of his hands in her hair, taking its weight, then running his fingers through it to comb it onto her shoulders.

When it all tumbled loose around her neck, he lifted it aside to kiss the sensitive nape area that raised delicious sensations all through her skin. A second later, his fingers had found the back fastener to her bra and were unhooking it. She drew a breath of heady excitement as he slipped the straps from her shoulders.

"Come to bed, Vanessa," Race urged huskily, and moved silently away from her.

By the time she had stepped out of the rest of her underclothes and come to the bed, he was already under the covers, waiting for her. The color of his dark eyes blackened as he watched her come to him, the silvering light from a streetlamp casting a white sheen over her nakedness.

She went into his arms with the eagerness of one coming home after a long absence. His mouth bruised its fierce welcome on her lips while his arms gathered her to him. She was fired by the heat of his passion and the burning warmth of his body, intertwined so intimately with hers. Race was knowledgeable about all the ways to excite her, all the pleasure points on her body that aroused her, and he exploited every one to the fullest.

When he mouthed the erect nipple of her breast, Vanessa moaned aloud in exquisite anguish. Her fingers raked their way into his hair to force him to stop this teasing, but he continued to rub his mouth over the hard peak of her breast without taking it.

"Talk to me, honey," he urged in a passion-thickened voice. "Tell me what you want . . . what you're feeling." When she moaned inarticulately again, he asked, "Do you still hate the way I make your body feel?"

"No," she admitted on a half-groan. "I love

what you're doing to me. But please don't torment me like this."

"It's heaven and hell all at the same time, isn't it?" Race described it accurately.

"Yes," Vanessa whispered on a tortured ache. "Love me, Race."

"Why?" He resisted her plea to end her searing misery.

"Because I want you," she admitted.

A fine tension seemed to leave him. Vanessa could almost feel him relax. "I've waited so long to hear you say that. I don't think you know how long," he muttered.

All that had gone before seemed nothing compared to the leaping fires he ignited in her. She was reeling and soaring, glorying in the crushing weight of his body, and inflamed by its hardness. Again and again he carried her to that high plain of ultimate satisfaction, until neither of them had the strength to attempt the journey again.

Exhausted, but more contented than she had ever been in her life, Vanessa lay comfortably wrapped in his strong arms. With each breath, she inhaled the warm, musky smell of him. She felt strangely boneless, without form or substance except through him. The feathering touch of his breath caressed her cheek.

"If this is all a dream, and you aren't really here in my arms, don't wake me," Race murmured.

"I don't think it's a dream," she assured him softly, ". . . unless we're both having the same one."

There was a long silence before he said, "We probably should go to sleep."

"I know," Vanessa sighed. "But I don't want to. If I go to sleep, then when I wake up it will be morning."

"That's the usual order," Race mocked gently. "First morning, then afternoon, then night, and morning again."

"That isn't what I meant." She guessed he knew that.

"You're afraid this won't last until morning," he accused softly.

"Yes." It was a quiet admission, reluctant and subdued.

"I have no intention of letting you go a second time, Vanessa," he stated. "This is where you belong, so you might as well start accepting it."

"But—"

"There aren't going to be any buts," he interrupted. "This time we're going to work out our problems. Now, go to sleep. We'll talk about it in the morning."

Vanessa wished she had his confidence. She wasn't as sure about the outcome as he was. It was sheer exhaustion that finally closed her eyes.

Chapter Nine

The intermittent ringing wouldn't stop. An irritated frown crossed her features as Vanessa tried to snuggle closer still to Race's hard, warm body and shut out the sound that was disturbing her sleep. But his hands moved her away from him and onto the mattress.

"It's the phone, Vanessa," he said in a voice graveled with sleep.

She stirred in protest, her frown deepening. The mattress sagged under his shifting weight. The shrill ring and his identification of its source finally penetrated her conscious mind. She dragged her eyes open just as Race picked up the extension on the small table beside the bed.

"Hello?" he answered dully, and wiped a hand across his face as if trying to rub out the sleep.

Little details began to register in Vanessa's mind: the hustling noise of traffic and people in the street below, the brilliance of the sunlight outside the window—and the hands of the clock dial pointing to nine-thirty. It hit her with belated force that she'd forgotten to set the alarm when they'd gone to bed last night. Her suddenly alert gaze flew to Race, sitting hunched over with tiredness, the covers loosely falling around his waist, and the telephone to his ear.

"Vanessa's asleep," he said into the mouthpiece, then glanced at her. One shoulder lifted in a slight shrug that indicated he hadn't known she was awake. "Who's this?" When he had his answer, Race lowered the phone and pressed it to his chest so the calling party couldn't hear his question to Vanessa. "Do you know someone named Pierre Bennoy—or something like that?"

"It's Peter," she realized, and grabbed for the phone but Race lifted it out of reach. "He's an interior decorator who works for me," she explained impatiently. "He's calling to find out why I'm not at the shop."

Race wouldn't give her the phone, carrying it again to his ear. "Vanessa won't be in the shop until around noon today. You'd better cancel whatever appointments she has this morning."

"Race, I can't do that!" she protested, and tried again to get the telephone from him, but he was hanging it up.

"It's all settled," he informed her.

153

Her mouth opened in sputtering indignation. It was several seconds before she could get her voice out. "I can't just arbitrarily take the morning off. I'm the boss. I'm supposed to be there."

"Look at the time," he reasoned. "Most of the morning is shot already. By the time you've showered, dressed, and had some breakfast, it will be practically noon anyway."

His logic tempered her anger but it didn't quell her irritation at oversleeping. "Why didn't I set the alarm?" Vanessa muttered in self-recrimination.

"Because . . ." Race turned to her, his arm sliding diagonally across her stomach to curve his hand to her waist. When he began leaning toward her, the sheer looming force of him pressed her backward until her shoulders were flat against the mattress. ". . . You were occupied in more pleasurable pursuits."

With a tug, he removed the pillow from beneath her head and tossed it aside. Anticipation flashed like white-hot lightning through her veins. Her lips parted with the first brush of his mouth across them, while her hands slid over the rippling muscles in his back to gather him in.

As the kiss deepened, his roaming hands began an arousing exploration of her feminine form, sparking the fires of her passion and pleasure. They were not driven by the urgency that had claimed them last night. There was time to enjoy all that led up to the the union of the flesh. And it seemed a stronger welding of desire and emotion because of it.

Cuddling afterward in his arms, Vanessa felt oddly refreshed and revitalized, instead of drained and spent. His lips moved against the tousled brown silk of her hair.

"Did you enjoy that?" Race asked with a trace of typical male pride for the role he'd played.

"Yes." She smiled secretly at the faint note of triumph and self-satisfaction in his voice.

His hold on her shifted, turning her so he could see her face. His gaze was three-quarter-lidded, lazy and warm in its study of her, a complacent glitter showing.

"Explain to me, if you can," Race challenged quietly, "what's wrong with morning sex?"

Vanessa stiffened. It was happening again—old disagreements were being resurrected to cast black shadows on the new accord they had found. She fought the raw ache that threatened to spread.

"Nothing," she murmured with lowered lashes to hide the hurt and resentment in her violet eyes.

Vanessa stirred in his arms, wanting out of them. Race didn't attempt to keep her there, letting her move away from him to sit on the edge of the bed, holding the covers around her. The silence lengthened from seconds into a minute. She could feel his eyes watching her as she pushed her arms through the sleeves of her robe.

"You didn't have that opinion when we were married." Race finally broke the tense quiet, not content with the nonargumentative answer she had given.

His unvoiced demand for an explanation

sharpened her resentment. She became irritated at his insistence the subject must be discussed at this time. It put an edge in her voice.

"I was younger then, and considerably less experienced," Vanessa defended her previous attitude. "I didn't think it was normal for a couple to make love as often as you wanted us to. I thought something was wrong with me because I did like it."

"So you accused *me* of being oversexed." His laugh was short and hard. "I don't think I'll ever understand the way a woman's mind works."

She turned, anger flaring as she stiffly buttoned her robe. "We're even, because I'll never understand how your mind works," she snapped. "Why are you insisting that we discuss this now?"

There was a slight narrowing of his gaze, measuring her. "If we can't discuss it now . . ." Race was reclining against a propped-up pillow, so very male and self-assured. His gaze made a slow rake of her robe to remind Vanessa that he knew intimately the body it concealed. ". . . After we've enjoyed making love to each other, when can we talk about it?"

His question threw her off balance. There was a certain logic to it that Vanessa found difficult to ignore. That very intimate side of their marriage had always been a raw issue between them. In some respects, it still was.

"All right." Vanessa turned on the bed to face him with faint belligerence. "Part of my attitude was caused by my lack of experience, but you're to blame for some of it, too."

"Me?" An eyebrow shot up in challenging surprise.

She breathed out a silent, angry breath at his slightly stunned and doubting look. It reeked of male arrogance and confidence in his own infallibility.

"Yes, you," she retorted. "You spent nearly ninety percent of your time in a fruitless search for that damned oil and gas." Unconsciously Vanessa revealed her jealousy toward his work. "When you did come home, all you wanted to do was make love. It wasn't long before I stopped feeling like your wife. I was just a free sex partner. It made it all seem cheap and degrading."

Frowning lines narrowed his eyes as he searched her features, made bitter by remembrance. "Are you serious?"

His disbelief nearly ignited her temper. Vanessa pushed off the bed in angry agitation, holding on to the lingering traces of pleasure she'd found in his arms moments ago to keep their discussion from exploding into a full-blown shouting match.

"It isn't something I'd lie about," she answered stiffly.

"And that's why you resented making love to me even when you enjoyed it," Race concluded in a musing tone.

"Yes." Her answer was flat, as Vanessa was unable to derive any satisfaction that he finally understood.

Perhaps because this had not been the true cause of her reason for leaving him. Race hadn't needed her—not then—and not now. He wanted her; he desired her; maybe he even loved her in his own way. Would she be content with that? That was the question forming in her mind that Vanessa wasn't prepared to face yet.

Since she wasn't ready to face it, she sought an excuse to end the conversation. "I'd better take my shower now if I expect to be at the shop by noon." She started toward the bedroom.

"Any objections if I shave while you shower?" Race asked. "Then I'll shower while you use the mirror to put on your makeup."

Since there was only one bathroom in her apartment, Race's strategy allowed both of them to make use of it at the same time without getting in each other's way. Yet Vanessa hesitated, struggling with the sensation of forced intimacy. She glanced at the wedding rings he had slipped on her finger last night. He had not forced her into accepting him. But daylight had cast shadows on a choice she had so willingly made last night. They created doubts and confusion.

"Sounds fine," she lied about her acceptance of his suggestion.

Preestablished patterns reemerged, bringing a moderately comfortable familiarity to this sharing of the facilities. Over the noise of the shower, Vanessa could hear his tuneless whistle while he shaved. It was something she hadn't realized she missed until she heard it.

When she stepped out of the shower, Race was slapping water on his face to rinse off the streaks of lather remaining on his smoothly shaved skin. She had the large bath towel wrapped around her by the time he straightened and saw her reflection in the mirror.

"It's all yours." Vanessa gestured toward the shower.

As they traded places, she felt a flicker of heat, that awareness of him as a lover, surfacing again. She grabbed for her toothbrush and bent over the sink to avoid looking at his hard, lean body when he stepped behind the shower curtain.

Steam was collecting on the outer edges of the mirror and gradually working its way to the center. When she started putting on her makeup, it took longer than normal because she had to keep wiping the mirror. It was something else she'd forgotten. Race finished his shower before she had her makeup on. It was virtually impossible to look in the mirror and not see all that rippling bronze flesh his towel was wiping.

"Feels like old times, doesn't it?" Race's glance met the reflection of hers in the mirror as he tucked the ends of the towel around his middle. There was a glint of mockery in his dark eyes to show that he was aware she had been admiring his male physique, albeit self-consciously.

"A little, yes," Vanessa admitted.

He walked up behind her, bringing their reflections close in the mirror. His hands closed on her shoulders, warmly possessive. The darkness of his eyes became like velvet, caressing her via the mirror.

"We had some good times," he reminded her,

although it wasn't necessary. "It wasn't all that bad."

"No." But Vanessa knew that the bad had been more recent than the good. She was also aware the freshness of that unpleasant time was receding.

Bending his head, he lightly brushed his mouth over her sensitive shoulder bone. "How much fresh grounds do you use to make coffee?" he asked when he straightened. "I'll get it started while you finish up."

"Two heaping scoops," Vanessa informed him, finding it difficult again to resist his brand of male appeal that seemed to want nothing from her but her acquiescence.

Race winked at her reflection, then moved toward the door to the bedroom, passing through her side vision as he left. Love seemed to tighten its hold on her heart. It was something she had to come to terms with, and either accept the situation or fight her way free again.

In an attempt to give herself time to think, Vanessa dawdled over the application of the rest of her makup. Race was moving around in the bedroom when she finally finished, no closer to a decision than before. There were so many risks involved in loving him, and the biggest of all was the potential for heartbreak.

As she entered the bedroom, her glance immediately sought him out. He was standing near the bed, tucking a faded plaid shirt inside the waistband of a worn pair of tan drill slacks. Vanessa was startled by the change of clothes, expecting to see him in the dark suit again. It prompted a searching glance of the room to find out where he had obtained them. An open suitcase sat on the unmade bed. Race reached inside it to take out a brown leather belt.

"Where did you get that?" Vanessa asked, her voice sharp with surprise.

Race glanced at the belt he was threading through the loops, frowning slightly as he misinterpreted her question, believing she was asking about the belt. "I've had it for years." He shrugged. "I don't remember now where I bought it. Why?" His glance in her direction was absently curious.

"I don't mean the belt." She frowned impatiently. "I'm talking about the suitcase. Where did it come from?"

"I had it in my truck," he replied with unconcern.

"But how did it get in here?" Vanessa persisted, certain that he hadn't left the apartment this morning.

"I carried it in here." Race gave her an amused look. "It doesn't have feet, so it couldn't have walked in by itself."

She flashed him an irritated glance, wondering if he was being deliberately obtuse. "I gathered that," she retorted. "My question is, when? I didn't see it in here."

"You obviously weren't looking. It was sitting there by your dresser." He flicked a hand toward the low walnut dresser drawers and fastened his belt. "I brought it in yesterday so I could shave and clean up."

"And you left it in here. You didn't take it back

to your truck." Her statements bordered on accusations.

"Obviously not." Race cocked his head to one side, studying her narrowly, as if trying to determine why she was upset.

"Then you were planning all along to spend the night with me, weren't you?" The discovery of his premeditation smarted. Last night hadn't been a spontaneous happening, the way she had thought.

"Let's say that I was hopeful," he qualified her remark. "You had been sending me signals, and I wanted to be sure of the message."

"I'm sure it's been received loud and clear," Vanessa murmured with a trace of bitterness as she walked stiffly to her closet. "I'm still a fool where you're concerned."

"You wanted me and I wanted you. Why does that make either of us a fool?" Race demanded with a frown in his voice.

Phrased that way, it didn't sound quite so bad. She sighed heavily, caught in the throes of confusion. "I guess it doesn't."

There was a slight pause, during which Vanessa felt the force of his gaze on her. "I'll pour us some juice and coffee while you dress," he said, not pursuing the subject.

She glanced over her shoulder as he walked out of the bedroom into the living room. If only he needed her, how simple everything would be, she thought wistfully. She slipped a camel-gold dress off its hanger and laid it on the unmade bed as she walked to the drawer containing her clean underclothes.

In less than five minutes she was dressed and walking to the kitchen. Race was seated at the small table, waiting for her. She sat down in the chair opposite his, where a cup of coffee steamed next to a glass of orange juice. She sipped at the latter.

"What are your plans for the day?" Vanessa asked, since it seemed the most subtle way of finding out if he intended to see her this evening.

"I have a couple of things I need to get done at the office." Race finished his juice. "I imagine it's going to be just as difficult for you to get away as it will be for me to work a honeymoon into my schedule. But we've already been that route once, so I don't suppose it matters if we skip it this time around."

He spoke so calmly, so matter-of-factly, that it was a full second before the import of his words made an impact on her. She was briefly paralyzed by them. Her silence drew a questioning glance from Race.

"We can keep the wedding simple this time— just invite a few close friends," he added. "I think Dad would like it if we had it at the house, unless you want a church ceremony again."

"What are you saying?" It was all coming at her too fast.

A faintly bemused smile touched his mouth as he reached across the table to take her left hand. "I'm saying that I want these rings on your finger *legally*. We should be able to arrange for blood tests, a license, and a minister by next weekend, don't you agree?"

"I suppose, but . . . ." She wanted to voice her

doubts, only nothing came out as her gaze clung to him in a silent appeal for time.

A darkening expression wiped the bemusement from his features. "What is it, Vanessa?" There was a hard bite to his question, a demand to know the reason behind her hesitation.

"Don't you think you're rushing things?" She made a weak attempt to reason with him.

"No, I don't." He released her hand, withdrawing from the contact with her and studying her with accusing dark eyes. "But you obviously do."

"I'm just not as sure as you obviously are that marriage would work for us." It seemed to Vanessa that all the concessions had to come from her. Race hadn't changed—in any respect. He still didn't need her. "I can't see where things are any different than they were four years ago."

Sudden anger darkened his eyes to an ebony black. "Damn you, Vanessa," Race muttered under his breath. "You complain that I didn't treat you like a wife. Why don't you try walking by my side instead of attempting to emasculate me?"

Her eyes widened in shock at his accusation. "I don't do that," she protested.

"Like hell you don't." The line of his mouth was thin and hard. "I've got as much pride as the next man. And I don't like it when the woman I love doesn't believe I can provide for her. But you can't resist throwing past failure in my face, can you?"

"It hardly matters," Vanessa inserted impatiently, because she hadn't even been thinking about his present financial straits, "since I have my own business and can take care of myself."

"That's right," he snapped. "Wave your success under my nose." His lip curled in bitter sarcasm. "But you didn't achieve it alone. You had help, which is more than I ever got from you or my father."

"I'm aware that you never received financial help or encouragement from either myself or your father," she admitted. "We both tried to change you, and that was wrong. I know better than to try this time."

"But you're still hung up on my risky business, aren't you?" Race accused, bringing his anger under an iron control. "Chances are, my future will never be financially secure. I'll always be gambling what I've got on the next well. That's the breed of the cat."

"I know that." It was something she had accepted, but Race didn't give her an opportunity to say it.

He pushed his chair away from the table and stood up, leaving his full cup of coffee untouched. "I want you, Vanessa," he stated, towering above her. "But I'll be damned if I'll get down on my knees and beg you to marry me. You either love me enough to spend your life with me—however rough it might be—or you don't. It's your decision to make. I love you, so I've already made mine." Race took a step away from the table, then paused to look back at her. "If it takes you more than a couple of days to make up your mind, then your answer will be no. If I haven't heard from you by Monday, don't bother to call."

When he turned his back on her, Vanessa opened her mouth to stop him from leaving. A little voice reminded her that she had claimed she needed time to think it over. Race was giving it to her, so she closed her mouth on the words of love and marriage that would have brought him to her side.

There was a numbness to her limbs when she stood up to follow him into the living room. Instead of exiting the apartment, Race headed for the bedroom. Just for a second, Vanessa couldn't think why.

"I'll take my things so I won't have to come back for them." He threw the explanation in her direction without actually looking at her. His voice sounded unnaturally taut, strained by the effort of keeping all emotion out of it.

She stood in the center of the living room, seemingly rooted to the floor while she listened to the noises he made packing his suitcase. Pale and a little frightened, Vanessa watched him come out of the bedroom and approach her, the suitcase gripped in one hand. His gaze seemed to bore into her when he stopped in front of her.

"I left a check on the dresser for the back alimony I owe," he said roughly, his mouth twisting in a harsh attempt at a smile. "I don't want you to think that I asked you to marry me to get out of paying it, but I'd cash it today, if I were you. There might not be enough money in the bank to cover it if you wait until Monday."

"I don't need it," she murmured tightly.

"Look at it this way." His mouth remained in its crooked line, bitter and mocking. "If your answer is yes, you can pretend it's a wedding present from me to you. And if it's no, it's payment for two nights of room and board." His gaze ran over her, as if remembering the other "services" that had gone along with it.

Vanessa stiffened to hide the stinging hurt his remark carried. "Don't make me feel cheap, Race." There was a husky throb in her low voice.

"If I could make you feel anything, I'd make you love me." The rumbling tautness in his voice made it sound like a threat.

His hand hooked itself behind her neck and pulled her roughly to him. The digging pressure of his fingers forced Vanessa to arch her head back while his mouth bruised her lips with a punishing urgency, grinding them against her teeth until she tasted blood.

Then she was released as abruptly as she had been taken. The room spun dizzily for a second before she was able to focus her gaze on the width of his shoulders as Race walked out the door. A second later, he was gone and she was staring at a closed door. Something wrenched at her heart, almost tearing it away. In pain, she moved numbly to a chair and sat down.

This was her chance to think, so why couldn't she? It seemed as if she had been sitting in the chair for only a few minutes when the phone started ringing. At first Vanessa ignored it, not wanting to talk to anyone until she had reached a decision on Race's ultimatum. The sheer fact that he had issued such an ultimatum seemed to prove that he didn't need her—that she wasn't really necessary to his future happiness.

It suddenly occurred to her that it might be Race calling. He could be having second thoughts about the hardness of his stand that allowed for no compromise. She grabbed for the telephone, and carried the receiver eagerly to her ear.

"Hello? " Her anxious response was met by silence. "Hello?'

"Vanessa?" A man's voice came back, but it belonged to Peter Benoit at the shop.

Her hope faded. "Yes."

"I was just about to hang up," he explained the initial silence. "I wouldn't have bothered you, but I have to know whether you are intending to come in at all today. I can't cover your appointments and mine, too."

"I'll be in," she murmured vaguely.

"When?" Peter questioned. "It's past noon and you've got a one-o'clock on your calendar for today."

His assertion of the time jolted Vanessa out of her daze. "It can't be that late."

"I beg your pardon, but it is." He sounded patiently amused.

"I'll be right there." She didn't bother to wait for a reply as she hung up the phone.

Chapter Ten

By the end of the day, Vanessa felt mentally and emotionally depleted. There was an ache inside that wouldn't go away. She glanced at the telephone on her desk, wanting to reach for it and dial Race; but for the hundredth time, she didn't.

The door to her office was open. Something moved by it, drawing her attention. Peter was peering around the frame, a bright twinkle in his eyes. Ever since she had arrived at the shop shortly before one, there had been a knowing quality to the looks he gave her. Vanessa knew it all went back to Race answering the telephone that had wakened them this morning. And Peter was nearly eaten alive by curiosity because of it.

She wanted desperately to be alone, but she

suppressed the wave of irritation at his appearance. "Did you want something, Peter?" she demanded briskly.

"No." But he swung the rest of his body into view and she noticed the cup and saucer he was carrying. "But I thought you might be needing the benefit of a little stimulant right now." He entered her office without waiting to be asked and walked to her desk to set the cup and saucer down. "Some black New Orleans coffee, guaranteed to be weighted with caffeine."

"Thank you." Vanessa accepted it, fully aware it was merely an excuse to speak to her privately and satisfy his curiosity.

"I guess it should have been champagne." Peter settled his slender frame into the chair in front of her desk. She darted him a questioning look and he glanced pointedly at her left hand. "Aren't congratulations in order?"

It felt so natural to have the wedding rings on her finger that Vanessa had forgotten she was wearing them. "Not really," she partially denied his question, aware that she only had to give Race the answer he wanted for it to be true. "These are just my old wedding rings."

"And it was just your 'old' husband that answered the phone this morning when I called," Peter guessed.

"Yes." The alternative to a truthful answer was to pretend it had been some other man. Vanessa quickly decided against that.

"Is there a reconciliation in the wind?"

She hesitated a second too long before answering. The instant she saw his expression take on a smug look, she realized it.

"I don't know." Again it was the truth.

"Which means one of you is not too sure," Peter guessed—again accurately.

The telephone on her desk rang. Vanessa reached for it quickly, grateful for the interruption that allowed her to avoid comment. "Vanessa Cantrell speaking," she said into the mouthpiece, adopting her professional tone.

"Hello, Vanessa. It's Phillip."

His bright, cheerful voice triggered a series of memories, including his call to her apartment the other night which Race had answered. She guessed that his curiosity was running as high as Peter's.

"Hello, Phillip." She injected a lightness into her voice. "How are you feeling?"

"Fine, fine." It was obvious that he didn't want to talk about himself. "Well?" There was a wealth of expectant meaning in the single-word question.

"Well, what?" Vanessa attempted a laugh of confusion.

There was a full second of silence before Phillip spoke again, more hesitantly this time. "Race proposed to you, didn't he?"

"How did you know?" Surprise pushed the admission from her.

"We talked about it a few days ago and again when he answered your phone the other night," his father explained, then chided her, "which doesn't answer my question."

"I . . . haven't decided," Vanessa replied, then glanced at Peter, realizing she was answering his question, too.

"I don't understand." Confusion ran heavy in his voice. "That was quite a concession Race made."

Aware that Peter was unabashedly listening in, Vanessa didn't want the conversation to continue. "I'm sorry, Phillip, but I can't discuss it right now."

A heavy sigh came over the phone lines, filled with disappointment. "I guess it's your decision to make, but . . . if you want to talk to me about it—"

"I know," she interrupted gently before he could offer his willing ear. "Thank you, Phillip." But she couldn't confide in Race's father, since he had already related previous confidences to his son. There was an exchange of good-byes before Vanessa hung up the phone.

"So you are the one who isn't sure," Peter guessed.

"Yes, I'm *not* sure." Her irritation crept through despite her attempts to keep it out of her voice.

"You're wearing his rings, so you must love the guy," he concluded. "So what's holding you back?"

Vanessa waged a silent debate within herself before deciding to see Peter's reaction to her reason. "He doesn't need me."

He looked at her with a smiling frown. "If he didn't need you, he wouldn't want you back."

"You don't know Race." She sighed, a dejected

and rueful smile lifting the corners of her mouth.

"I don't have to know him," Peter countered. "It's human nature. Nobody wants to share their life with another person unless that person also satisfies some need within them. Now, whether he needs you the way you want to be needed, that's another question entirely."

Vanessa stared at Peter, slowly letting his remark sink in. As it did, the doubts began to glide away. Her expression began to take on a new glow.

"Your coffee is getting cold," Peter observed with the beginnings of another knowing smile.

"I don't think I need it anymore." She reached for the telephone and dialed the number of Race's company. When a woman answered on the fourth ring, Vanessa guessed it was either his secretary or an answering service. "I'd like to speak to Race Cantrell, please."

"I'm sorry, but he isn't here right now. May I take a message?" the woman inquired.

"This is Vanessa Cantrell. Do you know where he is or how I might reach him?" she asked, trying to contain her eagerness.

"Mrs. Cantrell." The woman's voice seemed to take on a friendly warmth of recognition. "Race did leave a message in case you called. He had to go to the drilling site in Assumption Parish. Unfortunately, there isn't a telephone where he can be reached, but I will be talking to him first thing in the morning. Do you want to leave a number where he can call you, or is there a message I can give him?"

"I'll be at my apartment." Vanessa gave the woman her telephone number in case Race didn't know it, but no message. It was one she wanted to give him herself. When she rang off, she looked up to find Peter shaking his head at her. "What's the matter?"

"I was just commiserating with you because you have to wait now for him to call you," he explained.

Her spirits dipped for a second when she realized how long it was until tomorrow morning, but they soared with a new decision. "I'm not going to wait," she stated. "There's nothing keeping me here. Carla's left for the weekend, and you're going."

"I am?" He arched a dark eyebrow.

"Yes, you are." Vanessa didn't make any attempt to straighten her desk as she rose from her chair, prompting Peter to stand as well.

A few minutes later, the shop was locked for the weekend and she was waving to Peter as she walked to her small sports car. The long angle of the sun flashed its fire on the diamonds of her wedding rings. Vanessa smiled at the prism of light they reflected as she slipped behind the wheel.

Evening traffic lengthened the driving time from New Orleans to Assumption Parish. Darkness had settled in when Vanessa neared her destination. A sigh of relief trembled through her as the car's headlights picked out the sign on the gate that read: "Boars Head #1." She had just about decided she'd missed the turn.

Negotiating the narrow, rutted road in the daylight hadn't been easy. Attempting it at night was definitely a challenge as the trees closed in, creating a black tunnel. Lights flickered through the moss-draped branches, becoming steadier as she neared them.

When she reached the clearing, floodlights illuminated the drilling platform and trailer like daylight. There were fewer trucks parked in front of the office trailer. Vanessa maneuvered her car into an opening between two pickups and switched off the motor.

As she stepped out of the car, she made the same mistake as before—her high-heeled sandals sinking into the marshy ground. She tried to find more solid footing, but there didn't seem to be any. A shadow loomed suddenly in front of her, the noise of the man's approach drowned out by the loud drone of a pump motor at the well site.

"Looking for somebody?" the man challenged.

"Race Cantrell. Is he here?" Vanessa dodged a buzzing mosquito flying around her face and took a futile swipe at it with her hand.

"In the trailer." The man in coveralls motioned over his shoulder.

"Thank you."

The heavyset man just nodded and moved out of her path, heading for one of the trucks. The muddy ground was like a water-laden sponge that sucked at her shoes, trying to pull them off with each step Vanessa took. The puddle of murky water at the base of the trailer's metal steps seemed larger. Vanessa eyed the distance and height to the first step and knew she'd never make it in one long stride.

Headlight beams from the departing truck swept over her as it reversed away from the trailer. With a sigh of defeat, she balanced herself on one leg while she slipped the heeled sandal off her other foot, then repeated the procedure to remove the other shoe. Mud oozed between her nylon-covered toes, but it was better to have dirty feet and torn stockings than to ruin a pair of shoes.

Holding the shoes by the heel straps in one hand, Vanessa used them for balance as she waded into the puddle where the warm, muddy water lapped around her ankles. When she was within reach of the metal handrail, she grabbed for it and hauled herself onto the steps. Her wet feet made the footing slippery, forcing her to climb the smooth metal steps slowly, when she wanted to run.

The anticipation for this moment had been building all during the long drive to the drilling site, until now it was at a fever pitch. Her heart seemed to be tripping over itself in high excitement as Vanessa reached for the door. An interior light spilled onto the steps when she opened it and stepped quickly inside, shutting off the outside noise when she closed the door.

Her eager gaze darted to the office side of the room, oblivious of the other two men in the trailer, and halted the instant she located Race. He was in a frozen stance by the table with the coffee urn. There was a hint of pallor beneath his sun-bronzed features as his gaze first locked with hers, then slowly traveled down her length.

The flush in her cheeks made her face glow with the inner fire that had hastened her to his side. Her eyes sparkled like dark amethyst crystals. The high Louisiana humidity had begun curling tendrils of hair against her neck.

With a soft, self-conscious laugh, Vanessa realized what a picture she made in her belted camel-gold dress, with muddy feet and shoes in her hand. "I'm simply going to have to invest in a pair of boots before I visit any more of your drilling sites."

The sound of her voice seemed to prove to Race that she wasn't a figment of his imagination, breaking him free of the motionless stance. Yet his expression continued to show strain, something raw and stark flashing in his dark eyes.

"You damned well better be here to tell me yes." There was a hoarse rasp to his voice, low and urgent in its aching roughness.

"Yes." Her voice went husky with emotion, too, as she gave him her answer.

Without consciously directing her feet, she was moving toward him. A mighty thaw seemed to tremble through him, shattering the cold grip uncertainty had kept him in. His long strides covered the distance more quickly than her light feet. His strong arms gathered her up, lifting her feet off the floor while his mouth crushed its hungry kiss onto hers.

Her arms were wrapped around his neck, holding him as tightly as he held her. A delirious joy swept her high, making her feel weightless and boneless, and on fire with a happiness more complete than she'd ever known. Neither of them heard the other two men in the trailer when they discreetly slipped outside.

As the long kiss ended, Race slowly let her feet touch the floor, while his arms maintained their tight hold. His fiercely possessive embrace was heady bliss as Vanessa kept her eyes closed to implant this moment forever in her memory. He buried his face in the curve of her neck, roughly mouthing her sensitive skin.

"I love you, Vanessa." His voice was choked with raw emotion.

"I love you, too, Race . . . just the way you are," she vowed. "I want to be with you—all my life. Rich or poor. It took me a long time to realize that it doesn't matter whether we have a roof over our head or not, as long as we're together."

A violent shudder went through him as he loosened his hold on her and lifted his head to look at her upturned face. His hands were trembling as they moved over her shoulders and back, as if reassuring themselves that it was really her.

"Do you mean that?" he asked in an aching whisper.

At first, Vanessa couldn't answer. She was staring in silent wonder at his strong male features. There was a vulnerable quality about them. More incredible than that, there were tears in his eyes. She curved a loving hand to his hard, lean cheekbone and caught the tear in the corner of his eye with her fingertip.

Race not only loved her, but he also needed her. It was there, written for her to see in the shimmer of tears in his eyes. How could she have ever doubted it? Vanessa was overwhelmed and humbled by the totality of his love.

"Yes, I mean that." There was no uncertainty in her reply.

With a groan, he kissed her again. This time, there was none of the desperate urgency that marked the last. His mouth moved in a slow, adoring fashion over the softness of her love-swollen lips, showing her the gentle side of equally powerful passion. She combed her fingers into the virile thickness of his dark hair, clinging to his kiss and making it her own.

Neither of them spoke for a long second afterward, content for the time being just to be in each other's arms. Vanessa let her hands wander over the sinewed muscles in his arms and shoulders, aware of their male strength and their protectiveness.

His breath was warm against her cheek, an invisible caress when Race spoke. "Don't make a mistake. I could never let you leave me again."

"I won't leave you—ever," she promised again. "No matter how rough and rocky the road gets." Vanessa attempted to lighten the intensity of the moment. "Which isn't to say that I won't complain sometimes. I probably will. But you are my home—and your love is all the security I need."

A glint appeared in his eyes, as if enjoying some secret joke. "Are you sure?" Race challenged lightly.

"Yes, I'm sure," she answered, a little puzzled.

He pressed a firm kiss to her temple, then shifted to curve her to his side, nestled under the crook of his shoulder. "Let's go over here and sit down."

He guided her to the desk and sat down in the creaky swivel chair behind it, drawing her crosswise onto his lap. His hand roamed familiarly over her hip, the curve of her waist, and lingered on the straining fullness of her breast. Then he ran a finger over her lips, tracing their outline, while his eyes watched with interest the way they trembled.

"This is much better, isn't it?" Race murmured.

The position contained so many physically disturbing influences that Vanessa found it difficult to think, let alone talk. But she rather enjoyed this kind of elemental communication, too, from the unyielding solidness of his chest to the hard columns of his thighs.

"Much," she murmured, kissing the forefinger that tantalized her lips.

His gaze continued to study her with a certain knowing quality in his look. A smile slowly spread its warmth across his mouth, dazzling her a little with its potent charm. She held her breath in heady anticipation of his kiss, but it didn't come. Instead he turned his attention from her. The chair squealed a protest when he swiveled it at an angle and reached to open a desk drawer.

"I have something for you," Race said, and took a long, fat envelope from the drawer. There was a definitely complacent glitter in his eyes when he handed it to her.

The envelope flap was unsealed. Vanessa darted him a bewildered glance as she opened and withdrew a many-paged legal document. It would take too long to read and decipher all the legal jargon, so she turned her gaze on Race.

"What is it?" she asked.

"Your security," he stated lazily. "Now I won't have to hear you gripe about it anymore, and I can get on with my wildcatting."

"My security? What are you talking about?" She frowned and looked at the document again, not understanding its significance. "And I already told you that I'm not worried about security," she added for emphasis.

"I'm not taking any chances," Race replied on a dry note. "This document represents a legal trust, whereby all the income from this well, Boars Head #1, will be protected solely for you, with provisions for an annual allowance. Which should keep you in jewels and furs for a few years."

For a dazed moment Vanessa could only stare at him while she tried to absorb the meaning of his announcement. "Are you saying . . ."—it was hard to get the words out—". . . that your well is a producer?" Immediately she frowned, because she had asked him the same question only a day ago. "You said the other day that it wasn't."

"It isn't my well. It's yours," he corrected. "So I wasn't exactly lying when I told you *my* well didn't test out."

"But you did find the big one," she realized. When he nodded an affirmative reply, she was speechless with happiness for him, knowing how long and how hard he'd searched. "You did it!" she cried, and flung her arms around his neck, accidentally crumpling the legal papers in her hand. "I'm so glad! It's what you wanted! Now you've made it!"

He took hold of her wrists and pulled her arms down. "It was the challenge of finding it I wanted," he said. "That's my reward, because I finally caught the carrot that's been dangling in front of me. Now it's yours, so you'll never have to worry about tomorrow again. You're financially secure for the rest of your life."

"It isn't important to me anymore." Vanessa tried to make him understand. "I can't let you give me the proceeds from this well—your well."

"It's too late now." He shrugged lightly. "That's an irrevocable trust—signed, sealed, and delivered to you. All I'm entitled to receive are my drilling costs."

"That isn't right," she protested.

"Yes, it is." Race smoothed a hand over her cheek and let it glide down to caress her neck. "It's never been the money for me. I just want to chase the rainbows. You know as well as I do that I'd pour all that money into another 'hole in the ground.'"

"But—"

He pressed a silencing finger to her lips. "No

buts," he stated firmly. "This strike has enabled me to get all the financial backing I need to develop the rest of this gas field. I'll be drilling thirty or forty more wells in this area with damned good odds of tapping this same capacity. My company is going to be rolling in money when they start coming in."

Vanessa relaxed, some of her concern for the cost of his generosity fading. She remembered now that wherever there was one well, invariably there were several more at close intervals.

"But I'm not going to stop looking elsewhere," Race went on, "just because I found it here. In the wildcatting business, you can be a millionaire one day and flat broke the next." He glanced at the partially rumpled document she was holding. "But you're going to be secure." He winked. "You can support me in my old age."

"Are you sure you wouldn't be too proud?" Vanessa mocked with a deliberately provocative glance. "Not too long ago, you wouldn't even let me buy you dinner. You swore you'd never accept anything from me."

"Yeah, but I can always pretend that it's really my money." He grinned.

"Chauvinist," she laughed.

"If you want me to eat my words, I will," Race declared, becoming serious. "Because my pride had a lot to do with our problems."

"I don't want you to eat your words," Vanessa replied, but her curiosity was aroused by his last remark. "And I don't think it was your pride as much as it was my blindness."

He shook his head in silent denial while his

fingers absently stroked her neck. "When you walked out on me four years ago, I wanted to come after you and beg you to come back. I needed you so much—but my pride was hurt. It wouldn't let me tell you how much I loved you—how much I needed you. It made me lash out and hurt you in childish vengeance."

"I did some hurting of my own." Vanessa remembered some of the cutting words she'd said to him. "You seemed so impregnable, Race, as if nothing ever reached you—not even me. At the time, I thought it was the money and security that I needed and that you weren't giving me. But that was never the real cause. I didn't think you needed me," she admitted at last.

"I need you," Race affirmed huskily. "My damned pride kept getting in the way. I swore I'd never come to you until I could lay a fortune at your feet. That's why I never came near you these last four years." There was a wry twist to his mouth. "It was quite a blow to my pride when you came here to tell me about Dad's heart attack and I was so broke I couldn't even afford the extra gasoline money to make the drive to New Orleans. I must have been a masochist to take you to my apartment that night."

"I thought I was one for going," Vanessa admitted. "Especially when I saw your neighbor and the souvenirs from other female friends strewn around your apartment."

"Were you jealous?" He tipped his head to one side.

"Insanely so. But that's also when I started realizing what I'd given up when I left you." A remnant of that jealousy returned. "If you really loved me all this time, how could you sleep with another woman?" It was a hesitant question, showing the hurt she'd felt.

"Vanessa," Race murmured, "haven't you learned the difference between making love and having sex? God forgive me, but I never loved any of them. I'm not even sure if I liked them. You are the only woman I love—the only woman I've ever loved. I made my own hell these last four years."

"I didn't realize how lonely I'd been without you until we were together again," she admitted.

"We aren't going to be lonely anymore," he promised, and brushed her lips with a kiss. "Will a soon-to-be-very-rich woman consent to be a poor wildcatter's wife?"

"Yes . . ." Vanessa sighed contentedly, and studied him with a dreamy look. "I'm very lucky. A wildcatter has to be the only man who would give his woman her own gas well."

A throaty chuckle came from him at her remark. "I have to admit that's true."

"Why didn't you tell me before?" she wondered aloud. "You said you weren't going to come to me until you could lay a fortune at my feet. But you didn't do it."

"I was afraid." His gaze searched her face with a vaguely desperate look. "I was afraid I would be buying your love. And I wanted you to love me, not my money.'"

"That's why you didn't tell me." Vanessa realized he'd been testing her.

"I was going to, but I changed my mind at the last minute," Race explained. "I had Dad and the bank's attorneys draw up all the papers, and signed them so I could give them to you."

"Phillip knew about this?"

"Yes." He nodded. "It was after I told him about this trust fund I was setting up for you that he mentioned you were having second thoughts about our divorce. That's when I knew I had to find out whether you loved me for myself—and not for the security I could give you. I was scared you wouldn't, so I had one drink to find the courage to see you. It took about a half-dozen before I could gather up the nerve to go to your shop."

"It was the first time I'd ever seen you drunk," she recalled, able to smile about the incident now.

"It's a wonder you didn't throw me out."

"You needed me."

"I always have. To tell you the truth, that morning-after was the first time I thought I had a chance of winning you back. It just stood to reason that if you were willing to look after me when I was falling-down drunk, then you had to care about me. That's why I was still at your apartment, because I had to find out how much."

"Now you know," Vanessa murmured, and moved to shorten the distance between their lips.

"Now I know," he agreed, bringing the conversation to a close.

Silhouette ❦ *Romance*

15-Day Free Trial Offer
6 Silhouette Romances

6 Silhouette Romances, free for 15 days! We'll send you 6 new Silhouette Romances to keep for 15 days, absolutely free! If you decide not to keep them, send them back to us. You pay nothing.

Free Home Delivery. But if you enjoy them as much as we think you will, keep them by paying the invoice enclosed with your free trial shipment. We'll pay all shipping and handling charges. You get the convenience of Home Delivery and we pay the postage and handling charge each month.

Don't miss a copy. The Silhouette Book Club is the way to make sure you'll be able to receive every new romance we publish before they're sold out. There is no minimum number of books to buy and you can cancel at any time.

This offer expires October 31, 1982

Silhouette Book Club, Dept. SBO 17B
120 Brighton Road, Clifton, NJ 07012

Please send me 6 Silhouette Romances to keep for 15 days, absolutely free. I understand I am not obligated to join the Silhouette Book Club unless I decide to keep them.

NAME_____

ADDRESS_____

CITY_____STATE_____ZIP_____

Silhouette Romance

IT'S YOUR OWN SPECIAL TIME

Contemporary romances for today's women.
Each month, six very special love stories will be yours
from SILHOUETTE. Look for them wherever books are sold
or order now from the coupon below.

$1.50 each

Hampson	☐ 1	☐ 4	☐ 16	☐ 27	Browning	☐ 12	☐ 38	☐ 53	☐ 73
	☐ 28	☐ 40	☐ 52	☐ 64	☐ 94			☐ 93	
Stanford	☐ 6	☐ 25	☐ 35	☐ 46	Michaels	☐ 15	☐ 32	☐ 61	☐ 87
	☐ 58	☐ 88			John	☐ 17	☐ 34	☐ 57	☐ 85
Hastings	☐ 13	☐ 26	☐ 44	☐ 67	Beckman	☐ 8	☐ 37	☐ 54	☐ 72
Vitek	☐ 33	☐ 47	☐ 66	☐ 84				☐ 96	

$1.50 each

☐ 5 Goforth	☐ 29 Wildman	☐ 56 Trent	☐ 79 Halldorson
☐ 7 Lewis	☐ 30 Dixon	☐ 59 Vernon	☐ 80 Stephens
☐ 9 Wilson	☐ 31 Halldorson	☐ 60 Hill	☐ 81 Roberts
☐ 10 Caine	☐ 36 McKay	☐ 62 Hallston	☐ 82 Dailey
☐ 11 Vernon	☐ 39 Sinclair	☐ 63 Brent	☐ 83 Halston
☐ 14 Oliver	☐ 41 Owen	☐ 69 St. George	☐ 86 Adams
☐ 19 Thornton	☐ 42 Powers	☐ 70 Afton Bonds	☐ 89 James
☐ 20 Fulford	☐ 43 Robb	☐ 71 Ripy	☐ 90 Major
☐ 21 Richards	☐ 45 Carroll	☐ 74 Trent	☐ 92 McKay
☐ 22 Stephens	☐ 48 Wildman	☐ 75 Carroll	☐ 95 Wisdom
☐ 23 Edwards	☐ 49 Wisdom	☐ 76 Hardy	☐ 97 Clay
☐ 24 Healy	☐ 50 Scott	☐ 77 Cork	☐ 98 St. George
	☐ 55 Ladame	☐ 78 Oliver	☐ 99 Camp

$1.75 each

☐ 100 Stanford	☐ 105 Eden	☐ 110 Trent	☐ 115 John
☐ 101 Hardy	☐ 106 Dailey	☐ 111 South	☐ 116 Lindley
☐ 102 Hastings	☐ 107 Bright	☐ 112 Stanford	☐ 117 Scott
☐ 103 Cork	☐ 108 Hampson	☐ 113 Browning	☐ 118 Dailey
☐ 104 Vitek	☐ 109 Vernon	☐ 114 Michaels	☐ 119 Hampson

$1.75 each

Silhouette Desire
15-Day Trial Offer
A new romance series that explores contemporary relationships in exciting detail

Four Silhouette Desire romances, free for 15 days!
We'll send you four new Silhouette Desire romances to look over for 15 days, absolutely free! If you decide not to keep the books, return them and owe nothing.

Four books a month, free home delivery. If you like Silhouette Desire romances as much as we think you will, keep them and return your payment with the invoice. Then we will send you four new books every month to preview, just as soon as they are published. You pay only for the books you decide to keep, and you never pay postage and handling.

Silhouette Romance

Coming next month from
Silhouette Romances

Daring Encounter by Patti Beckman

Glamour, daring, mystique . . . Lord Richard Templeton
had them all. And it was up to Andria to make America's
top race idol an offer he couldn't refuse.

Devotion by Anne Hampson

Caryl's harmless masquerade backfired when Brad
proposed to the wrong girl! Could she ever reveal herself
and win his heart for her own?

Time Remembered by Lee Sawyer

His family had sent her father into bankruptcy years ago.
But Sabrina couldn't deny the passion that engulfed her
when Jules took her into his arms.

Game of Chance by Donna Vitek

Jason was everything Kit had ever hoped for, except that
he was a gambler. Could she accept his profession, or
would she lose the gamble—and his love?

An Ocean Of Love by Elizabeth Reynolds

He called her a gold digger and a fraud! Then suddenly,
his attitude changed, and Jill found herself passionately in
love with a man she didn't even like.

Yesterday's Bride by Susan Tracy

After years of separation, Leigh wanted to avoid seeing
Jason again. But he lured her into his turbulent world, for
she was his *wife*!

**Look for *Search For Love* by Nora Roberts
Available in July.**

READERS' COMMENTS ON SILHOUETTE ROMANCES:

"I would like to congratulate you on the most wonderful books I've had the pleasure of reading. They are a tremendous joy to those of us who have yet to meet the man of our dreams. From reading your books I quite truly believe that he will someday appear before me like a prince!"

—L.L.*, Hollandale, MS

"Your books are great, wholesome fiction, always with an upbeat, happy ending. Thank you."

—M.D., Massena, NY

"My boyfriend always teases me about Silhouette Books. He asks me, how's my love life and naturally I say terrific, but I tell him that there is always room for a little more romance from Silhouette."

—F.N., Ontario, Canada

"I would like to sincerely express my gratitude to you and your staff for bringing the pleasure of your publications to my attention. Your books are well written, mature and very contemporary."

—D.D., Staten Island, NY

*names available on request